W9-CMI-776

Silver Moon Rising

Silver Moon Rising

Ethan J. Wolfe

FIVE STAR
A part of Gale, Cengage Learning

GALE
CENGAGE Learning

Farmington Hills, Mich • San Francisco • New York • Waterville, Maine
Meriden, Conn • Mason, Ohio • Chicago

LIBRARY OF CONGRESS CATALOGING-IN-PUBLICATION DATA

Names: Wolfe, Ethan J., author.
Title: Silver moon rising / By Ethan J. Wolfe.
Description: First edition. | Waterville, Maine : Five Star, a part of Cengage Learning, Inc. [2016]
Identifiers: LCCN 2016003822| ISBN 9781432832797 (hardcover) | ISBN 1432832794 (hardcover)
Subjects: | GSAFD: Western stories.
Classification: LCC PS3612.A5433 S55 2016 | DDC 813/.6—dc23
LC record available at http://lccn.loc.gov/2016003822

First Edition. First Printing: September 2016
Find us on Facebook– https://www.facebook.com/FiveStarCengage
Visit our website– http://www.gale.cengage.com/fivestar/
Contact Five Star™ Publishing at FiveStar@cengage.com

Printed in the United States of America
1 2 3 4 5 6 7 20 19 18 17 16

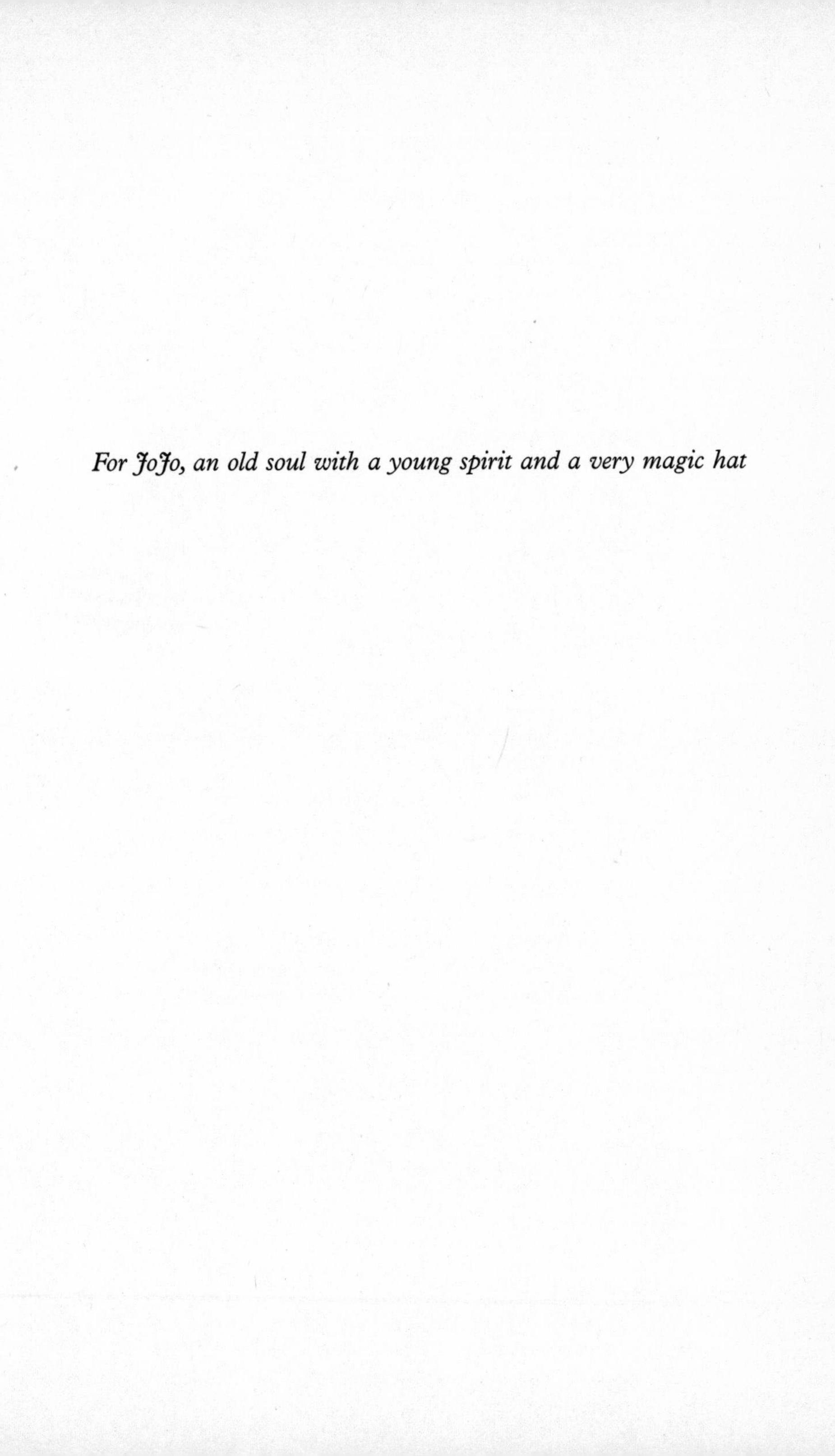

For JoJo, an old soul with a young spirit and a very magic hat

Chapter One

Alfred J. Wallace surveyed the dusty, bleak land surrounding the Overland Stage Coach way station where he awaited the noon coach bound for Denver, Colorado.

If ever God turned his back on a piece of the earth, it was this place. Harsh, mountainous, and unfit for man to live upon, yet live upon it man did. Wallace stuffed his fine briar pipe with tobacco and lit it with a wood match.

The station manager said the coach would be about thirty minutes late coming north from Gunnison. A scout rider said something about replacing a busted wheel on the road. Wallace was anxious for the coach to arrive. The journey to Denver would take long enough without added delays.

Wallace walked to the water barrel in front of the way station and used the ladle to take a few sips. The water was warm from the hot sun, but cut through the dust in his mouth.

He heard footsteps behind him and the station manager said, "Mr. Wallace, we have a hot lunch prepared while you wait. Should we set a plate for you?"

Wallace turned around.

"I'll be right there," he said.

He finished his pipe and then went inside the way station. At the table were the Mexican woman and her half-breed son, the two soldiers assigned to escort her to Denver, his personal assistant George Bell, and the old doctor traveling alone.

Wallace knew nothing of the Mexican woman and her son,

not why the army was escorting her or her reason for traveling to Denver, and he didn't really care enough to ask. The same could be said of the old doctor.

George Bell was a recent addition. Wallace hired him three months ago as his personal assistant when his longtime assistant died suddenly of what the doctors said was a heart attack. The duties weren't strenuous. Keep the horses and carriage ready, go to town for the mail and supplies, and accompany him to Indian land several times per month to distribute supplies and medicine, and once a month ride to the Cattlemen's Association in Denver to buy beef for the various tribes.

In the three months Bell had been with him, the man had done a fair job.

This was their second trip to Denver to buy beef.

And Wallace's last. He'd reached the age of sixty and his retirement from the Bureau of Indian Affairs. From Denver, he would buy the beef at auction using the government check sent to him from Washington, then ride the railroad east to his hometown in Maryland where he would live out his days in style and comfort.

Not from his pension of seventy-five dollars a month for sure, but from the forty thousand dollars in cash he had in the money belt he wore under his shirt. Stolen money from the beef contracts he secured over a period of twenty years. He never got greedy and only took tiny increments at a time, but over twenty years it added up to the tidy sum hidden in his money belt.

Wallace took a seat next to Bell at the table. The Mexican woman and her son sat at the far end of the table, but if you asked Wallace, he would have made them sit at a table by themselves. It was bad enough he had to ride in the same coach; he certainly didn't want to eat with them.

The station manager set a plate before Wallace and filled it with beef stew and cornbread. There was a choice of water, coffee, or buttermilk to drink. Wallace chose the buttermilk.

"How long you figure we'll be in Denver?" Bell asked.

"Three days or so," Wallace said. "Don't worry, you'll have plenty of time for drinking and whores."

The doctor, seated opposite Bell, looked up from his plate. "You know what the cure is for catching a whore's pox?" he said politely.

Bell looked at the doctor.

"It's quite painful," the doctor said.

The soldiers came in from the rear door and dusted themselves off with their gloves.

"Would you care for some hot food?" the station manager asked them.

"That would be good," a soldier said.

They sat with the Mexican woman and her son.

"How long to reach Denver?" the Mexican woman asked.

"Three days' ride if there are no more breakdowns," the station manager said.

The Mexican woman nodded politely. "Thank you," she said.

The station manager set plates and dished out food for the soldiers.

"Best eat while you can," the station manager said. "You won't reach the next way station until eight o'clock tonight."

The back door opened again and the station scout came in. "Stage will be here in about ten minutes," he said. "Soon as the driver and his passenger eat, and I change out the horses, you'll be on your way."

Deets was a crusty, older man going on twenty-five years as a driver for Overland. He started back in fifty-four in Missouri when the roads were filled with danger at every turn from Indians and bandits.

Today, the only real danger came from broken wheels and

mud after heavy rains washed down from the mountains.

The company still insisted on a man riding shotgun, but the last time a bandit attacked a stage he drove was back in seventy-one, some eight years ago.

Deets figured to drive a stage until they retired him or went out of business. His shotgun rider, an experienced hand named Tully, packed away more food than any man Deets had ever known, yet kept skinny as a rail.

Once they ate their fill and the horses were changed out, Deets told the passengers to mount up if they were going. Fortunately, he had just the one passenger, so there was plenty of room.

The one passenger, a squirrely businessman from Santa Fe, had a problem.

"I might be able to tolerate riding with a Mexican, but sharing a coach with an Indian is out of the question," the passenger said.

"Capacity is eight," the station manager said.

"I know what the capacity is," the passenger said. "I'm talking about dignity. A white man does not ride with Indians."

One of the soldiers stepped forward. "The woman and her son are under the protection of the US Army," he said.

"That's fine and dandy for the US Army, but I won't ride with them," the passenger said.

"Suit yourself," the soldier said.

"What does that mean, sir?" the passenger asked.

Once all bags had been loaded onto the top of the coach, Deets looked at the man staying behind.

"Ain't he coming?" Deets asked one of the soldiers.

"No," the soldier said. "He decided to suit himself."

"More room for everybody else," Deets said. "Well, let's get rolling."

Wallace sat next to a window and watched the scenery roll by hour after hour. Without glass in the coach door windows, the dust blew inside and caused him to cough every few minutes. He considered rolling down the dust flaps, but that would have darkened the coach, making the ride even more depressing than it already was.

After four hours, the driver stopped for a fifteen minute rest and to allow the passengers to relieve themselves.

The last two hours of the ride were accomplished after dark. The moon was full and the road was clearly visible. Wallace lowered the window flap and a soldier did the same on the other side, and most everybody snoozed until the coach stopped at the next way station.

Torches illuminated the Vail, Colorado, way station. Smoke rose up from a brick chimney. Flickering lights shone in the windows.

All appeared nice and comfortable.

But no one was there to greet them.

Deets and Tully saw right off something was peculiar. Usually the station manager and scout would be outside to greet them when they pulled in, but tonight no one was there.

Deets and Tully got down.

"Everybody stay inside for a moment, folks," Deets said.

"Is something wrong?" a soldier asked.

"Don't know," Deets said.

"We're armed," the soldier said.

"All right, you two soldier boys come out," Deets said.

Tully gently nudged Deets. "No horses in the corral," he whispered.

The soldiers exited the coach and stood next to Deets.

"What is it?" one of the soldiers asked.

"Too quiet," Deets said.

Tully cocked the shotgun. "Let's go see why," he said.

They started to walk to the way station cabin, and suddenly three men with pistols drawn came around from behind the coach.

"That's far enough," Emmet Lang said.

The soldiers, Deets, and Tully froze in place.

"Good. Now be so kind as to drop all weapons," Lang said. "And know that three cocked pistols are aimed at your backs."

Tully dropped the shotgun, then his pistol. Deets drew his Colt revolver and tossed it to the ground. The soldiers opened their flap holsters, removed their pistols, and tossed them away.

"George, bring him out," Lang said.

Inside the coach, Wallace looked at George. George had his gun drawn and aimed right at him.

"What is the meaning of this?" Wallace said.

"You heard him. Out," George said.

Wallace opened the door and stepped out, followed by George.

"I demand to know the meaning of this," Wallace said.

"Get the money belt," Lang said.

George reached for Wallace's pants.

"Get your hands off me," Wallace said. "I am a government agent."

Lang grinned at Wallace. "What you are is a thief and a bigger one than me, I might add. Now remove the belt."

"I see that you leave me little choice," Wallace said.

Wallace reached for his pants, quickly removed the .32 caliber pistol hidden in his coat, and cocked the hammer.

George shot Wallace in the chest and the old man stumbled backward, looked at George, and then fell dead to the ground.

"Was that necessary?" one of the soldiers asked.

"No, it wasn't," Lang said. He looked at George. "We agreed there would be no killing."

"He drew on me," George said. "What was I supposed to do?"

"That pea shooter couldn't kill a chicken," Lang said. "Get the belt."

George knelt before Wallace and removed the thick money belt. He opened the flap and stood up, grinning. "All here. All forty thousand."

Lang looked at the soldiers, Deets, and Tully. "You see, Mr. Wallace was stealing money from his beef contracts intent for the Indians," he said. "Only he did it with pen and paper instead of a gun."

"I know you," Deets said. "You're Emmet Lang the outlaw, and these must be your gang. I seen the posters at the station in Denver."

George looked at Deets, and then he and the other two men opened fire and killed the soldiers, Deets, and Tully.

"Are you all crazy?" Lang shouted. "There's no need for . . ."

George struck Lang on the back of the head with his Colt pistol, and Lang slumped to the ground.

"We ain't taking your orders no more, Emmet," George said. "You come up with a great plan and we're all rich now, and we thank you kindly."

"We better go," Curly Johnson, gang member, said.

"What about them?" Smiley Hatfield, another gang member, asked and looked at the coach.

"Get rid of the old man," George said. "Leave the woman in the coach. We got some use for her."

"Okay, but I get to drive the coach," Johnson said gleefully.

Chapter Two

Emmet Lang woke up next to a pool of dried blood. The blood wasn't his, but a gathered pool from the five nearby dead men. In the moonlight, the blood appeared quite black.

He stood up slowly and felt dizzy and slightly nauseous. Dried blood crusted on his right cheek. He walked to the horse trough and stuck his face into the cool water, counted to ten, and came up for air.

He felt better. Not good, but better.

His hat and gun were on the ground and he retrieved them. George and the others left the soldiers' guns and the shotgun where they fell.

They took the coach and horses.

Lang holstered his Colt, put his hat on, and inspected the five dead men on the ground.

There had been a woman and child on the coach, and no sign of them anywhere now. The outlaws either took them with them, or they were hiding in the cabin.

He walked to the cabin, stepped onto the porch, and the wood creaked under his weight. Lang was a tall man, about six-foot-one in an age when five-seven was average height for a man. His boots added inches to that height.

Lang was about to open the door when he paused and drew his Colt pistol. The woman, if she was inside, could have a rifle or shotgun aimed at the door just waiting for him to walk through it.

He shoved the door in hard and stepped out of the way.

Not a sound came from inside. Lang entered the cabin and sighed heavily. Earlier, he and the boys tied the station manager and scout to the wood chairs at the table and gagged their mouths.

Both men had been shot through the heart.

There was no sign of the woman and her child. The boys must have taken them or let them go and they ran away.

Taken them was more likely.

For what reason? he thought. They had the money, horses, and coach and would be tens of miles away by sunup.

There was a coffee pot still warm on the woodstove. Lang grabbed a tin cup, filled it, and went to sit on the porch. His tobacco pouch and paper were still in his shirt pocket. He rolled a cigarette and lit it with a wood match.

He looked at the dead men on the ground.

They'd turned a simple robbery into a mass murder.

The beauty of his plan was that Wallace had no one to complain to about being robbed of the money he cheated the Indians out of. It wasn't like he could go to a marshal and swear out a warrant on the embezzled forty thousand; he'd wind up in prison himself.

The killings were done out of meanness and no other reason except for madness. A man kills for no reason has got to be crazy, just plumb crazy.

Seven dead men.

He couldn't dig seven graves, but two large holes should do, he figured.

Or he could leave the bodies where they were, and the stage coming through around noon tomorrow could deal with them.

Didn't seem right, leaving them for the buzzards and worms that would surely get at them by morning.

Lang finished his coffee, then took a lantern to the shed out back and found a shovel. The dirt beside the cabin was soft so he got to work digging.

By midnight, the seven bodies were buried in two deep holes side-by-side.

Exhausted, Lang returned to the cabin for something to eat. The pantry was filled with supplies, but he was too tired to cook much. He opened a can of beans and heated them on the woodstove. When they were hot, he put them on a plate and ate them with cornbread that had been baked fresh that afternoon.

He found a bottle of rye whiskey and washed the meal down with a few swigs.

Then he toppled onto one of the beds in the back room and fell asleep with his boots still on, he was so tired.

CHAPTER THREE

Rosa Escalante hugged her son tightly as the stagecoach raced along the moonlit road. She knew why the men kept her aboard and that it would be ugly. She hoped and prayed they would tie her son up away from them, or kill him, so that he didn't have to watch his mother being raped.

The coach raced along for quite awhile, and then quite suddenly, whoever was driving brought the team of horses to a stop.

Rosa held her son and shielded his face in her bosom.

The man she knew as George opened the door.

"Last stop. Everybody out," he said.

Rosa closed her eyes and held her son.

"You deaf?" George snarled. "I said out."

"Go to hell," Rosa said.

George grabbed the boy. He fought like a tiny hellcat. George was forced to put the boy down with a hard right fist.

The other two men reached into the coach and grabbed Rosa by the hair and yanked her out to the hard ground.

"This can go hard or this can go easy, that's up to you," George said. "But it's going to happen, so resign yourself to that fact and save yourself some bruises."

Rosa stared at George.

"Don't rip my dress," she said.

The other two men laughed.

"And my son. I don't want him to watch," Rosa said.

"Don't worry about the boy. He's sleeping," George said.

Curly Johnson was last to take a turn behind the coach with the woman, and when he was finished, he came back around and said, "What do we do with her now?"

George and Hatfield were passing a bottle of whiskey around. After George took a hard swig, he said, "Tie her and the half-breed in the coach. Next one comes along will find them."

Johnson took the bottle and took two long swallows. "I been studying on something," he said.

"What's that?" George said.

"We left Emmet alive," Johnson said. "He'll look for us."

"Curly's right," Hatfield said. "Emmet ain't likely to take what we did lying down."

"Emmet's on foot and likely to stay that way for a while," George said. "We got us forty thousand dollars. By the time Emmet gets a horse, we'll be halfway to Texas, boys."

"Still, we ought to go back and kill him," Johnson said.

"And grab some of the supplies they had in the cabin," Hatfield said.

"You want to go back and take on Emmet in the dark, go right ahead," George said. "I'm riding till daybreak to put some distance 'tween me and that stage."

"All right, we'll ride the night, George," Johnson said. "Just remember that money ain't yours, it's ours."

"Course it is, boys," George said. "Split three ways instead of four is more money for us. Now let's ride."

Johnson and Hatfield exchanged glances. It was obvious they didn't trust George, but they were almost as afraid of him as they were of Lang.

George stood up, walked to his horse, and quickly mounted the saddle.

"Coming?" he said.

Chapter Four

Lang awoke before daybreak. He rolled out of the bunk stiff and sore and with a slight headache from the lump on the back of his head. He ran the indoor pump and stuck his head under the freezing cold water to clear out the cobwebs of sleep.

He figured he had about six hours or so before the next stage arrived. He went through the supplies, and after building a fire in the woodstove, made a breakfast of beans and bacon, coffee, and leftover cornbread.

While the breakfast cooked, Lang removed a pillowcase from a pillow and gathered up as many supplies as the case could hold. From the weapons closet, he selected a Winchester rifle, two boxes of ammunition for it, and two boxes for his Colt Peacemaker.

In the desk by the window, he found three hundred dollars in folding money and stuck the bills into his shirt pocket.

There was a one gallon canteen by the water pump and he filled it, then ate quickly and was on his way shortly after sunrise.

Being on foot, choices were limited. He could take the road to the left and likely encounter the coming stage, go right and put some distance between him and the way station, or take to the hills.

He decided on right. The stage, upon discovering what had happened, would probably stay put for a day or more. A rider would head back to Gunnison to wire a marshal, and by the time a marshal arrived, it would be at least four or five days.

Lang could travel the road and stay out of sight until he could formulate a plan.

Maybe find a ranch or something where he could buy a horse and then ride the hell out of Colorado and head south to God's country.

By noon, he had come about six miles. The breakfast had worn off and his stomach had that empty feeling of wanting more. He decided to walk another hour before finding a place to build a fire and rest a bit.

Maybe a mile farther down the road, Emmet spotted the abandoned stagecoach just sitting there. The team of horses was gone, scattered or ridden off with George and the others.

Lang approached the coach with caution. The Winchester was cocked and ready when he peered through the window and saw the woman and the boy. They were hogtied back-to-back with gags in their mouths, but still alive.

The woman faced him. Her eyes were ablaze with fear and hatred as he opened the door.

Lang set the Winchester aside and withdrew the long knife on his belt from its sheath. The woman glared at him.

"I won't hurt you," he said. "I'm just going to cut you and the boy loose."

He reached in and sliced the ropes from the woman's wrists and legs, and did the same for the boy.

As Lang replaced the knife in its sheath, the boy pounced on him in a fury. He couldn't weigh more than eighty pounds, but his bony fists stung Lang's face and chest.

Lang grabbed the boy's arms to restrain him.

"Lady, I mean you and the boy no harm," he said. "Tell the boy to stop."

Rosa snapped at the boy in Apache, and the boy quieted down, lowered his fists, and looked at Lang.

Lang released the boy and stepped back.

"George and the others left you here like this?" Lang asked.

"Yes," Rosa said. "After they violated me like the pigs they are."

Lang sighed. "I'm sorry, ma'am," he said. "It wasn't supposed to be this way."

"No?" Rosa said. "How was it supposed to be?"

"I . . . look, I'm going to find a shady spot and make something to eat," Lang said. "Why don't you and the boy have some food with me?"

Rosa stepped out of the coach and placed her arm around her son's shoulder.

Lang glanced around and spotted a wide tree about thirty yards off the road.

"Over there," he said.

Lang walked to the tree and set the pillowcase and rifle against it. He gathered some stones and made a circle, then filled it with dry brush and twigs. With a match, he made a fire.

Rosa and the boy watched Lang from the road. The man went about the task of building a fire and cooking food as if he was used to living in the open. After a while, she could smell the beans and bacon cooking in a fry pan and her empty stomach growled. So did her son's.

She took the boy's hand and led him to Lang. He was sitting against the tree, smoking a rolled cigarette.

"Change your mind?" he asked.

"My son is very hungry," Rosa said. "If you could spare some for him, I would be grateful."

"Just so happens there are three tin plates and I made enough to fill them all," Emmet said. "And there's some day-old cornbread wrapped in paper."

Rosa looked at the three stacked tin plates. Three spoons rested on the top plate.

"There's coffee if you like," Lang said.

There were two tin cups beside the fire.

Rosa lifted the pot by the handle, using her skirt as a potholder, and filled both mugs. She handed one mug to Lang.

"Sit," he said. "I won't hurt you or the boy."

Rosa spoke to her son in Apache and he sat on the ground.

"He half-breed?" Lang asked.

"Yes," Rosa said.

"What's his name?"

"Joaquin."

"That's Mexican, isn't it?"

"So is he, half anyway," Rosa said.

"Food's ready," Lang said. "Does he know how to use a spoon?"

"He knows."

Lang dished out three equal portions of beans and bacon and they ate in silence for a while. The boy, skinny as he was, ate every scrap on the plate and a good-sized hunk of the cornbread.

Afterward, Lang rolled a cigarette and smoked while drinking a second cup of coffee. "What's your name?" he asked Rosa.

"Rosa. Rosa Escalante."

"I'm sorry you got mixed up in all this," Lang said. "Do you have any bags still on the stage up top?"

"Yes," Rosa said.

"I'll leave you some supplies to last you until the next stage comes along, or at least a posse," Lang said. "Should be tomorrow."

"Where are you going?" Rosa asked.

"West and away from here."

Rosa looked west at the mountains in the distance.

"Why?" she asked.

"Because I don't fancy swinging from a rope for murders I didn't commit," Lang said. "Go get your bag and I'll leave you some supplies to hold you over."

Rosa took Joaquin's hand and they walked to the stagecoach. She climbed on top, unstrapped her satchel, and tossed it to the ground. She checked the canteen on the seat, then told Joaquin to wait for her, and took the bag to Lang.

"Two cans of beans, two cans of fruit, a few chocolate bars, and a can of condensed milk," Lang said. "I'll leave you some water if you have a receptacle."

"There is a full canteen of water on the driver's seat," Rosa said.

"I'll be on my way then," Lang said. "I'm sorry for your trouble. If I ever meet up with those three again, I'll be sure to kill them for what they did to you."

Lang gathered up the pillowcase and Winchester and walked west toward the mountains.

Rosa watched him for a while and then returned to the stagecoach.

Chapter Five

Even the damned foothills of the Rockies were strenuous to cross, especially carrying a full sack and loaded rifle.

But Lang needed distance between him and the way station, so he pushed hard until close to nightfall. He gathered firewood and built a campfire to cook some supper. Water was at a premium, so Lang made just two cups of coffee.

As supper cooked, Lang rolled a cigarette, sat against a tree, and stared at the mountains in the distance. The Rockies were a handful in summertime and treacherous in the winter months.

Fortunately, he had no plans to stick around and wait for the cold weather.

The coffee came to a boil before the supper was cooked, and he added some to a tin cup and waited for it to cool a bit before taking a sip.

He should have known better than to team up again with George Bell and his two friends, but to Lang's figuring, the only way to avoid spilling blood was to have superior numbers.

A way station manager and his scout weren't apt to put up much of a fight when faced with superior firepower, and neither would a coach driver or his shotgun rider.

Something must have happened to George during the eighteen months he spent at Yuma Prison for robbing and beating a cardsharp who took his last dime in a Flagstaff saloon. The cardsharp died from his wounds, and the judge gave George three years, but paroled him after eighteen months for good behavior.

That was five months ago. When Lang heard George was out, he looked him up in Tucson with the proposition for the Wallace job.

Lang met Wallace's assistant in a Denver saloon. He was an older, nervous type, who played a few hands at the Metropole Saloon where they met. When the assistant found out who Lang was, he bought him a drink and told him his story.

Alfred Wallace, Indian agent for the government, was a thief who stole from the Indians. Wallace planned to retire on his sixtieth birthday with his stolen money. Money that couldn't be reported to the law. The assistant claimed the amount to be forty thousand dollars.

Originally, the assistant was to be in the stagecoach, but he up and died a month later. Luck brought Lang George Bell right out of Yuma. Broke and without prospects, George agreed to try to work for Wallace for the three months necessary. George could read and write and knew his multiplication tables. Wallace hired him on as his assistant after George rode to Wallace's house looking for work.

When Lang told George the job required two additional men to pull it off, George recommended two fellows from Yuma who got out the same time as he did. While George went to work for Wallace, Lang went to look them up.

Curly Johnson and Smiley Hatfield were of a hard sort. Small-time criminals who never made a big haul and were willing to do whatever it took to gain riches. In this case, Lang told them, just being there as a show of force was all that would be necessary. They seemed as afraid of him as they were of the law, and Lang figured to have no trouble from either of them.

The four met several times a month to discuss Lang's plan leading up to the day of the robbery.

George played his part right well and taking control of the

way station was no problem at all. An old station manager and his scout were far from gun men, and it wasn't their money or even that of the stage line that was being robbed.

Lang never suspected George would betray him the way he did. Off and on, they'd ridden together since the end of the war.

Yuma must have filled George full of hate and revenge for him to murder those men in cold blood the way he did.

Lang didn't know if it was planned or spur of the moment, but that didn't matter to the dead men he buried.

He checked the fry pan, and the beans and bacon were ready. He filled a plate and ate with his back against the tree.

Thing of it was, would the law come after him, or George and the others? Probably both if they caught up with George and he tried to make a deal with the law. A lesser sentence in exchange for cooperation and names, and the only one George had to give was Emmet Lang.

He needed a good horse with a decent saddle if he was going to put distance between him and the way station.

A marshal probably had access to dogs, and bloodhounds could track a man clear across Death Valley and back again.

Lang finished eating and rolled another cigarette. He finished the coffee while he smoked and continued to watch the mountains.

He hated to leave the woman and her son alone at the stagecoach, but they would be picked up tomorrow by the next stage or the law. Either way, they would be fine.

She was a pretty woman with dark, alluring eyes and hair as black as charcoal. She didn't deserve what George and the others did to her, but she appeared as strong-willed as an Arizona rattlesnake and would survive. So would the boy.

What was her name?

Rosa.

What the hell were they doing on that stage?

No matter.

Lang put the fire out so it wouldn't be seen after dark. He used the sack full of goods as a pillow and fell asleep with the Winchester cradled in his arms.

Chapter Six

In his ten years of driving an Overland Stage, Joe Butler had never encountered anything like what waited for him at the way station north of Gunnison. As they made the approach, his shotgunner, Willie Jones, remarked that he didn't see the scout rider as they made their approach.

That in itself wasn't too unusual. The scout could be feeling poorly or out doing something else at the moment.

Butler didn't let that bother him until he pulled the stage into the way station and no one was there to greet them and the corral was empty of fresh horses. Then the hairs on the back of his neck tingled.

Jones felt it, too.

"That scatter gun loaded?" Butler asked.

"It's of no use unloaded," Jones said.

"Let's see what's going on around here," Butler said.

Butler and Jones got down from the driver's seat and Butler opened the coach door. There were four passengers onboard.

"Folks, it will be just a few minutes before you can come out," he said. "Nothing to be alarmed about, so just sit tight."

Never in a hundred years did Butler think he would find two freshly dug graves at the side of the cabin.

"Do you think it's Woody and Don?" Jones asked as they looked at the two graves.

Woody was Woodrow Curry, station manager, and Don was Donald McFee, station scout.

"I'm sure it is, but that ain't what's spooking me," Butler said.

Jones looked at Butler.

"If that's Woody and Don, then who dug them graves?" Butler asked.

"Got to be whoever took the horses," Jones said.

"Yeah," Butler said. "Best get the folks and supplies inside."

The four passengers were rightly upset at the delay and downright angry at being told they would have to spend the night at the way station.

"The beds are comfortable, and we have enough fresh supplies to last a week," Butler told them. "I know it's a real inconvenience, but under the circumstances I don't know what else to do except follow company procedure."

A businessman wearing an eastern dude suit spoke up. "We could ride on to where we're going, that's what else we could do," he said, angrily.

"I can't endanger the lives of passengers," Butler said. "Until we know what's happened here, moving on will just have to wait until I know for sure it's safe. In the meantime, everybody get comfortable. Anybody that's handy in the kitchen is welcome to prepare us all a hot meal."

Butler nodded to Jones, and the two men left the cabin and walked to the stage.

"Put the team in the corral," Butler told Jones. "Let them rest for a few hours and then grab the scout's saddle, pick the best horse in the bunch, and ride to Gunnison and tell the sheriff what's happened here. He'll probably wire Denver for a marshal. Do you think you can make it by nightfall?"

"I can ride the road in the dark," Jones said. "Besides, it's near a full moon tonight. I'll make it and see you in the morning."

"Best take a rifle from the gun cabinet," Butler said.

"What do you think happened here?" Jones asked.

"Beats me, Willie," Butler said. "All I know is it isn't good."

Chapter Seven

Colonel William West sat behind his desk and read the arrest papers on the renegade Apache, Grey Wolf.

West was in his twenty-second year in the army and had fought under Grant in the Great War between the states. Afterward, he requested frontier duty, as he wanted to see the frontier before it was all settled and tame. He planned to do a few more years and then retire to the family home back east in Baltimore. His three daughters would all be of marrying age by then, and he planned to teach at the academy. He was ten years a widower, and he might even remarry. He figured to do his final three years at the outpost in Denver.

But this morning, his full attention was on the murdering savage Grey Wolf. Since before the war, the army and the law had been after him for his crimes. Some said Grey Wolf came out of New Mexico, other claimed Arizona and Texas. Nobody really knew, as he'd never been captured before. That he was captured at all was a small miracle, even if it was more by luck than design.

Grey Wolf had a band of forty renegades, and they'd traveled the western states unimpeded by the law or civilization for twenty years. He and his band raided farmers, settlers, and even attacked small patrols of soldiers. No one knew where his hideout was located, or if there was more than one. No one knew for sure what had driven Grey Wolf to his renegade life.

The arrest papers said Grey Wolf was to be transported to

Fort Collins where a team of army interrogators would interview him before a trial date was set.

West looked up from the papers.

"Runner?" he said loudly.

The office door opened and a corporal stepped inside.

"Yes, Colonel?"

"Find Captain Nelson and have him report to me immediately."

"Yes, sir."

Ten minutes later, Captain Nelson knocked on the door, opened it, and stepped inside. "You sent for me, Colonel?"

"Are you prepared to transport Grey Wolf?" West asked.

"The transport wagon is prepared, Colonel, as is my detachment of eight," Nelson said. "We leave right after breakfast."

"Do you think eight is enough for the two-day ride?" West asked.

"He's only one man, Colonel."

"Make it twelve men, Captain."

"Yes, Colonel."

"Good. I'll join you for breakfast."

An hour later, West stood outside his office and watched the detachment leave the fort.

Captain Nelson took the point, followed by six soldiers in a formation of two. Directly behind them was the transport wagon with the prisoner Grey Wolf in chains, and behind that rode another six soldiers in a formation of two. The wagon was driven by one of the outpost scouts, a Navajo called Moses.

West's three daughters suddenly appeared next to him.

"What's happening, Father?" the eldest daughter asked.

"Nothing to worry about," West said. "Nothing to worry about at all."

Chapter Eight

Lang awoke stiff as a board. He stretched and felt bones creak and crack and make noises he'd never heard from his body as a youth.

He made a fire to boil some coffee and rolled and smoked a cigarette while the coffee percolated. He removed a can of peaches from the sack and opened it with his knife. He drank the sweet syrup first and then ate the peaches. Then he finished the coffee, rolled and smoked another cigarette, and was on his way.

He walked west and covered ten miles by noon. He rested for thirty minutes and ate another can of peaches and some jerked beef. He didn't make coffee, but did sip some water.

Lang knew the country well. There was a mountain stream close enough to reach by nightfall. A few days after that, he would be in the mountains, cross through a pass, and maybe reach a ranch near Craig where he could buy a horse.

He knew he should push on, but Lang allowed himself the luxury of smoking another cigarette first.

Jones returned with the sheriff and two of his deputies by noon.

Abel Tweed had been sheriff of Vail going on twelve years. It was a fairly easy job to handle. Drunks on Saturday night, mostly. Any bar fights he left to his much younger deputies to handle.

Butler and Jones showed Tweed the gravesite on the side of the cabin.

"Curry and McFee?" Tweed asked.

"Assume so," Butler said. "We ain't dug it up yet. We figured to wait for you."

Tweed looked at his deputies. "Get some shovels from the shed."

Captain Nelson called for noon rest after five hours of steady riding. The road to Fort Collins was well traveled and easily traversed, and a great place for an ambush. Beset on both sides by the foothills of the Rockies and the Rockies themselves, the road was the only way to the fort, so Nelson had the men on high alert.

The men built a fire and prepared a hot lunch with coffee.

Nelson took a plate and cup and sat against a tree to eat.

Moses approached him.

"What about the prisoner?" he asked.

"Have four men let him out to take a piss and eat if he wants to, but keep him shackled at all times," Nelson said.

"Seven bodies," Tweed said. "My God."

"This don't make no sense at all," Butler said.

"What do we do about all this, Sheriff?" one of the deputies asked.

Tweed looked at his deputy. "Ride back and wire the marshal in Denver," he said. "Tell him what happened and request he get here pronto."

The deputy nodded and walked to the corral for his horse.

"What about us?" Butler asked.

"Everybody just stay put for now," Tweed said. "Me and my deputy are going to take a look around."

★ ★ ★ ★ ★

Grey Wolf eyed his captors with total disregard. To Grey Wolf, the soldiers were no better than a pile of horse shit. His disdain showed on his face as he urinated against a tree.

A soldier approached him with a plate of food.

"Speak English?" the soldier asked.

"No, not a word," Grey Wolf answered in perfect English.

"Smart ass," the soldier said. "I hope I'm there to see you swing."

"Doubtful," Grey Wolf said and took the plate.

Chapter Nine

Late in the afternoon, Lang began to get the strange feeling that he was not alone. He hadn't seen a living soul since he left Rosa and the boy yesterday afternoon, yet the feeling plagued him as he walked along the foothills.

Open country could do that to a man, put him ill at ease about being alone. Not that Lang had a problem with being alone; he'd been so for most of his adult life. It was being alone on foot when the law was mounted and could easily run him to ground that bothered him.

He would feel better once he reached the Rockies, where it wasn't so easy for a horse to follow and there was lots of good cover.

If he kept up a good pace, he could reach the base of the mountains and the stream by dark.

Nelson checked his pocket watch and estimated one hour of daylight remaining. He called a halt to the squad.

He called his sergeant and told him to make camp. A fire, hot meal, and then a two-man watch until morning.

"The savage?" the sergeant asked.

"Let him out to eat, but under watch, then lock him up for the night."

"Yes, sir."

Moses approached Nelson.

"Want me to ride ahead and scout the road?" Moses asked.

"No need. I've traveled this road a hundred times," Nelson said.

"Never with the likes of this one," Moses said.

"He's one man, Moses," Nelson said. "He'll be caged, and I'll have a guard on him all night. Grab some food and relax."

"Yes, Captain."

After eating, Nelson assigned guard duty and instructed them to keep the fire burning all night until breakfast.

It was a warm night with a bright moon, and Nelson placed his bedroll away from the fire. He watched the stars until he felt his eyes grow heavy, and then he drifted off to sleep.

Tweed and his deputy reached the abandoned stagecoach by nightfall. The nearly full moon was up, and it was easily seen on the road.

They stopped at the coach and dismounted.

"They took the horses," the deputy said.

"Well, I didn't think they pushed it all this way," Tweed said.

"Now what?" the deputy asked.

"It's too late and too dark to try and pick up their trail," Tweed said. "All we can do is head back and grab us a hot meal."

Chapter Ten

The attack came when the near full moon was at its zenith. It was swift and vicious, and Grey Wolf's renegades showed no mercy to their victims.

The first two soldiers they took out were the two sentries patrolling near the wagon where Grey Wolf was incarcerated. The renegades were experts at guerrilla fighting and had little trouble sneaking up behind the sentries and slitting their throats. Once the two were dispensed with, the entire band of forty renegades descended upon the sleeping soldiers with tomahawks and turned the camp into a river of blood. They split skulls and took scalps. The attack was over in a matter of seconds.

They spared Captain Nelson and Moses for Grey Wolf. They banged them up a bit, but left them alive and fully intact.

They found the keys to the cage and shackles and freed Grey Wolf.

Grey Wolf stood before Nelson and looked at the man. Nelson, not a short man, was surprised at how tall and powerful the Apache was compared to himself. Nelson realized that he'd just never taken a good look at the man before.

Grey Wolf showed Nelson nothing in the way of emotion. He simply stared at the captain as if looking through a pane of glass.

Then, and it happened so fast Nelson didn't see it coming, Grey Wolf hooked Nelson's legs with his right foot and brought Nelson to his knees.

The renegades whooped loudly.

Grey Wolf held up his right hand and they fell quiet.

"They call you Captain Nelson," Grey Wolf said. His voice was deep and rich in tone.

"Yes," Nelson said.

Grey Wolf untied his belt and urinated on Nelson's uniform.

"I call you dog," Grey Wolf said.

A renegade gave Grey Wolf a tomahawk.

Nelson showed he was no coward. He held eye contact with Grey Wolf right up until the moment Grey Wolf split his skull open.

Grey Wolf turned to Moses.

"Ride to the fort and tell the soldiers what you have seen here," Grey Wolf said. Then he knocked Moses unconscious with the tomahawk.

Lang found the stream of cool mountain water just before dark. He drank his fill and set up camp on the embankment. He built a fire and made supper. He was pretty sick of beans and bacon, but that was all he had for hot food at the moment.

Since water was readily available, he made three cups in the coffee pot.

Maybe tomorrow he would take a bath in the creek and maybe catch a fish or two, but tonight he just wanted to eat and then sleep.

After eating, Lang rolled a cigarette, drank his coffee, and watched the moon rise in the sky. It was waning, but still close to full and appeared almost silver in color as it rose above the mountains.

If he had to, he could find a pass through the mountains to put some real distance between him and the posse he knew would be coming, but he needed a horse and saddle to really widen the gap.

He could ride to the Hole in the Wall pass in Wyoming and hide out for months until he figured things out properly.

If he had a horse and saddle.

The sky was clear and millions of stars twinkled overhead. Lang rolled another cigarette and smoked, watching the stars.

And then for no apparent reason, he felt that strange sensation of being watched again. He stood up and walked to a tree to relieve himself and scanned the immediate area.

The moon was bright enough for his night vision to see clearly, and he saw nothing or nobody.

Lang returned to the fire and used the sack for a pillow.

In his saddlebags, he had thirty-five-hundred dollars, his entire wealth. He wondered if George took the time to go through the bags and find the money tucked into a folding wallet.

There was also his silver pocket watch he purchased in Santa Fe, New Mexico Territory, a few years back for thirty-five dollars. Besides his black ivory-handled Colt revolver, it was his most prized possession.

There was no use crying over it now. The money and watch were gone.

Come morning, he would hit the mountains.

Chapter Eleven

George, Smiley Hatfield, and Curly Johnson were eating in the Metropole Emporium in Denver. George was smart enough to know they had to lie low and not cause anyone to look in their direction for a while, so they didn't gamble at the tables.

George had a keen eye, especially for the law. Across the large gambling hall, three lawmen were eating supper. He thought it odd that they would be eating at nine o'clock in the evening, but then, so was he.

George recognized their badges. The star inside the circle, the badge of a US Marshal. He'd killed several sheriffs in his time, but never a marshal.

Well, now was not the time to start.

George and the boys were drinking rye whiskey with their meal. As George filled his glass, he noticed the telegraph operator from Western Union enter the emporium and rush to the marshals' table.

He spoke a few hurried words.

The oldest of the three marshals nodded and the operator scurried out of the emporium.

A minute later, the oldest of the three marshals stood up and left.

"Boys, we best ride out of town right after we eat," George said.

"We ain't visited the whorehouse yet," Johnson said.

"Whores can wait," George said. "We best make tracks for

Hole in the Wall pronto."

"But it's nighttime," Hatfield said. "We can't ride at night."

"We can and we will," George said. "Soon as we pick up some supplies."

"What's spooked you, George?" Johnson asked.

"I just seen something I didn't like," George said. "Finish up."

Marshal John Cox read Sheriff Tweed's telegram twice. The operator stood by the marshal and waited for him to give instructions.

"Marshal?" the operator finally said.

Cox lowered the telegram.

"Reply?" the operator asked.

"Send the reply to Sheriff Tweed," Cox said. "Tell him I'll leave first thing in the morning."

The operator knew better than to ask and simply nodded.

Cox pocketed the telegram, left the telegraph office, and walked along the wood plank sidewalk to his office. He paid no attention to the three trail-weary cowboys who exited the Metropole Emporium just as he passed the swinging doors.

The cowboys watched Cox carefully to see if he would turn around. When he didn't, they mounted their horses and rode away.

Cox went to his office and lit the lantern on his desk. The coffee pot on the woodstove was still hot, and he filled a mug and took a seat.

The door opened and his two deputies entered the office.

"What's going on, Marshal?" one of the deputies asked.

Cox removed the telegram from his pocket and set it on the desk.

"From Sheriff Tweed over in Vail," he said. "They found the passengers on the Overland Stage murdered and buried at the way station."

"The doctor was on that stage, wasn't he?" a deputy asked.

Cox nodded. "Along with the Mexican woman, her son, and two soldiers assigned to protect her."

"Good God," a deputy said.

"I'll be leaving at first light," Cox said.

"Alone?" a deputy asked.

"I need you two to stay here, monitor the office and telegram traffic, and keep the peace," Cox said. "One of you ride over to the fort in the morning and see Colonel West. Tell him two soldiers were killed at the way station."

"How long you figure to be gone?" a deputy asked.

"Two weeks, maybe more," Cox said. "Right now I'm going home and get some sleep. I'll see you before I go in the morning."

George stopped at the general store at the edge of town that stayed open late and purchased supplies.

Hatfield and Johnson waited by the horses.

George came out with two large sacks and they distributed their contents among their saddlebags.

"That marshal didn't pay us no mind, and I aim to keep it that way," George said. "Let's ride."

Cox entered the house he'd shared with his wife for twenty years and lit the lantern on the table in the hallway. As was his custom, he removed his gun belt and hung it on one of the coat hooks beside the door.

He entered the den, filled a glass with rye whiskey, and sat behind the desk. Johanna was gone four years now, and he still couldn't get used to how quiet the house was at night without her in it.

Their two daughters married well and moved back east. One

to a Boston doctor, the other a Philadelphia lawyer, and he didn't see them much anymore.

Consumption, the doctors called it. A polite way of saying tuberculosis. When she was first inflicted, they went to the large clinic in Minnesota. The doctors there did their best, but she grew worse, and the last six months of her life were spent in Glenwood Springs, where the high altitude was supposed to help her lungs and prolong her life.

It didn't.

She died while he sat reading to her from the Bible, her favorite book, and from her favorite passage.

He should sell the house and find small quarters suited for a man living alone, but he wanted to wait until he retired in three years when he reached thirty years as a marshal. He'd started in eighteen fifty-two as a junior deputy in Arkansas and worked his way up to a senior marshal in the service. When the war came, he was out west in the territories and missed the whole thing, but the war might have been safer. He had to battle bandits, murderers, thieves, and Indians in territories where he was the only law for a hundred square miles.

He'd been shot three times, stabbed six, and damned near scalped more times than he cared to remember, and all to bring law and order to a lawless country that didn't want him there in the first place.

Sometimes, it seemed as if he'd wasted his life. All these years, and still seven people could be murdered in the blink of an eye and for no apparent reason.

Weary, tired to the bone of his job and the evil men do to each other, Cox finished his drink and went straight to bed.

Chapter Twelve

Lang was up before sunrise and built a campfire to make coffee and cook breakfast. While coffee boiled and the beans and bacon cooked, he drew some fresh water from the stream and filled the gallon canteen.

Lang ate slowly and watched the sun come up over the mountains. It was a beautiful sight to see the peaks come alive with a quick burst of light and color. He rolled a cigarette and lingered over coffee until the sun had warmed the earth.

He didn't have his razor or a bar of soap or a change of clothing, but he felt the need to wash the sweat and grime off his body. He removed all his clothing and waded into the stream up to his knees. The water was cold, but there was no other way to do it so he dove under quickly to take the sting out of it.

The center of the creek was the deepest point, but that was only a depth of about five feet. Lang swam and waded about for a bit until he felt clean, then he stood up and turned to shore.

He was a bit shocked to see Rosa on the bank of the creek with her son, Joaquin, by her side. She was aiming his cocked, Colt revolver at him.

"We need food," she said.

"There's some left in the pan," Lang said. "Help yourself and make some more if you like."

Rosa spoke to her son in Apache and the boy started to remove his clothing.

"What's he doing?" Lang asked.

"If I lower the gun, will you hurt us?" Rosa asked.

"If I was interested in hurting you, I'd a done so back at the stage," Lang said.

Rosa lowered the Colt, uncocked it, and replaced it in the holster.

Joaquin was completely nude. He looked at Rosa and spoke in Apache.

"He wants you to come out of the water," Rosa said.

"Well, I'm a little exposed here," Lang said.

"I don't understand," Rosa said.

"Turn around and I'll come out," Lang said.

"Oh," Rosa said and turned her back.

Lang emerged from the stream, grabbed his underwear and pants, and quickly put them on. He stayed shirtless to let his chest and arms air-dry.

Joaquin slowly waded into the stream and stood in two feet of water and didn't move.

Lang turned to Rosa. "What's the boy doing?"

"Fishing," Rosa said. "Apache style."

Lang sat to put on his socks and boots. "Without a rod and hook?"

Joaquin moved suddenly and swiftly, reaching into the water with his hands. He snared a fish and quickly tossed it to shore, then went motionless again.

"I'll be damned," Lang said.

By the time he stood up, Joaquin had another fish on shore.

"Looks like he could do that all day," Lang said.

"He can," Rosa said.

A third fish flew onto shore. Rosa shouted to her son, who emerged from the stream and went to his clothes. As he dressed, he spoke to Rosa.

"He says to give him your knife and he'll clean the fish," Rosa said.

Lang strapped on his holster, removed the knife, and handed it to the boy.

"I'll make some fresh coffee," Lang said.

Colonel West visited the infirmary where Moses was resting after being examined by the doctor.

"Morning, Colonel," Moses said when West entered the infirmary.

"How are you feeling, Moses?" West asked.

"Headache is all. Doc said I'll be fine."

"I've wired the outpost in Fort Collins and asked for additional men," West said. "I'd like you and another scout to lead the sixty men I'm sending after Grey Wolf."

"I'll do it, Colonel. I owe him this bump on my head, but we won't catch him," Moses said. "Not this time."

"You're probably right, but we have to try. It's our duty," West said.

A runner entered the room and saluted West. "A deputy marshal here to see you, sir," he said.

"I'll be right there," West said.

Lang rolled a cigarette and sipped coffee as the boy fried the fish in the pan.

"Why did you follow me?" Lang asked Rosa. "I told you a stage would be by the next day."

"I need you to take us with you," Rosa said.

"With me?" Lang said. "You don't even know where I'm going. Plus, I'm on foot. The stage will take you back to . . ."

"No more coaches," Rosa said.

Lang stared at her for a moment.

"The soldiers on the stage, they were protecting you," he said. "Why?"

"I am a witness for the army," Rosa said. "And Joaquin. They were taking us to Fort Collins."

"Witness to what?" Lang asked.

"You will take us with you?" Rosa asked.

"I'm not doing a damn thing unless I know what's going on first," Lang said.

Rosa sighed and then unbuttoned the top two buttons of her blouse. She lowered the blouse past her right shoulder and turned her back to Lang.

"Do you know what this is?" she asked.

Lang looked at the burn mark etched into the right shoulder blade. It was the Apache mark of a captive woman; a brand like you'd brand cattle.

"Who?" he asked.

"Apache raiders," Rosa said.

"Who married you and sired the boy?" Lang asked.

"The one called Grey Wolf," Rosa said.

For a moment, Lang was speechless.

"Grey Wolf," he said. "Well, that's just great. That's all I need is that murdering bastard on my trail, as if the law ain't enough. Sorry lady, I got troubles of my own."

"We will follow you," Rosa said. "You will not see us, but we will be there. We will steal your food at night and when Grey Wolf comes for us, he will take you, too, and you will never know it. Isn't it better to know when he is coming than to not?"

Lang stared at Rosa as she replaced her blouse.

Joaquin spoke in Apache.

"He said the fish is ready," Rosa said.

Chapter Thirteen

West entered his office to find a deputy marshal having a cup of coffee.

"Colonel West?" the deputy marshal asked.

"Yes. Who are you?"

"Deputy US Marshal Alexander, Colonel."

"You must have something important to tell me," West said. "Unless you rode all this way for the coffee."

"Two soldiers were killed at the way station between Vail and Denver, Colonel," Alexander said. "Marshal Cox wants to know if they're yours."

West sat behind his desk and sighed heavily. "They're mine. What happened?"

"We don't know, Colonel. Marshal Cox left this morning to find out."

"I'd appreciate a wire as soon as you find out," West said.

"Yes, Colonel," Alexander said. "Colonel, what were they doing on the stage? Marshal Cox asked me to find out."

"Protecting the wife of Grey Wolf and his son," West said. "She was to give testimony to the army at Fort Collins."

"Grey Wolf?"

"Yes," West said. "However, yesterday he escaped. Tell that to the marshal."

"The boy cooks good fish," Lang said, grateful to be eating something other than beans and bacon.

"Joaquin was raised Apache," Rosa said. "He can live off the land while you would starve."

"Good, because I won't feel so bad when I leave you behind," Lang said.

"You will have to kill us, because that is the only way we won't follow you," Rosa said.

"I told you, I need to get a horse and ride to Hole in the Wall in Wyoming to hide out for a while," Lang said. "It's bad enough the law will come after me. I don't need the likes of Grey Wolf on my ass."

"So you will not kill us," Rosa said.

"No, of course not," Lang said.

"Grey Wolf will find us, and when he does, he will," Rosa said.

Lang stared at Rosa.

"I will take a quick bath in the stream before we go," Rosa said. "I brought a bar of soap in my satchel."

"It's not very private for a lady," Lang said.

"Try living with the Apaches," Rosa said.

Chapter Fourteen

After six hours of hard riding, Cox arrived at the way station around one in the afternoon. His forty-nine-year-old back ached the way it never did ten years ago. There was stiffness in his legs that he never remembered having as a young man, but he was no longer a young man, so the aches and pains were to be expected from being in the saddle for so long a time.

Sheriff Tweed, Joe Butler, and Willie Jones greeted Cox when he dismounted.

"How are you doing, Abel?" Cox asked as he dismounted.

"Damndest thing I've ever seen, John," Tweed said. "We got a hot lunch on the stove. I'll tell you what I know while we eat."

Cox looked at the stagecoach parked in front of the cabin. "The passengers?" he asked.

"Inside. We held them over. I didn't know what else to do," Tweed said.

Lang had to admit that for so small a boy, Joaquin kept pace like a grown man. Rosa had little trouble keeping up as well, even when the terrain took a stiff upward turn as they neared the Rockies.

Shortly before noon, by the sun's placement in the sky, Rosa spoke to her son in Apache, and the boy went running off in a different direction.

"What did you tell him?" Lang asked.

"Hopefully, you will see before we stop to rest," Rosa said.

Lang watched the boy disappear over a hill.

"Should we wait for him?" he asked Rosa.

"No. He'll catch up."

"Be another hour before we stop," Lang said.

"He'll be fine," Rosa said. "Don't worry."

Close to one in the afternoon, Lang selected a flat stretch of ground to rest and make a fire.

"Where's the boy?" he asked.

"He'll be along," Rosa said. "I'll gather some wood."

Once the fire was going, Lang measured for three cups of coffee in the pot and set it to boil.

"I best go look for him," Lang said.

"No need. He's here," Rosa said.

Lang turned. Walking up the hill was Joaquin, and he was carrying a yard-long, snowshoe hare.

"How the . . . ?" Lang mumbled.

They watched the boy until he arrived with the hare, and then Joaquin spoke to Lang in Apache.

"He wants to borrow your knife to skin the hare," Rosa said.

After lunch, Cox and Tweed rode to the abandoned stagecoach.

Cox inspected the scene carefully. Women's clothing was tossed about on the ground haphazardly. There were footprints of three men and one woman. From the tracks in the dirt, it appeared the three men had their way with the woman before they rode off northeast toward Denver.

The horses from the stage were scattered to the south, but what didn't make sense was there were seven tracks when the team consisted of only six horses.

A fourth man had arrived on foot. He, the woman, and what appeared to be a small boy walked away traveling northwest.

None of it made a lick of sense.

"I'm curious about something," Cox said. "Let's follow the

team they scattered for a bit."

Cox and Tweed rode south for about an hour and found the seven horses grazing in an open field of tall grass.

One of the horses, a large black male, had a saddle on it.

Cox and Tweed dismounted.

"How do you figure this?" Tweed asked.

"Could be there was a fourth man who did this, and he went afoot for some reason," Cox said. "That male seems tame enough, let's check out the saddle."

They approached the male, and while Tweed held the reins, Cox removed the saddle and saddlebags.

Under the saddle, carved into the leather, was the name Emmet Lang.

"Look at this," Cox said.

Tweed read the name.

"You don't suppose that's Lang, the outlaw?" Tweed asked.

"Got to be him, but this isn't how Lang operates," Cox said.

He went through the saddlebags and found a silver pocket watch with Lang's name inscribed on the back, and thirty-five-hundred dollars in folding money in a flap wallet.

"I'm not understanding any of this," Tweed said.

"Let's take the male back with us," Cox said.

The hare was perfectly cooked, and they ate nearly all the meat off the bones. Joaquin had skinned the hare perfectly, and Rosa saved the pelt in her satchel.

"When you snuck up on me in the creek and said you wanted the food, that was a lie," Lang said. "This boy could feed an army."

"I had to say something," Rosa said. "Or would you rather I threatened to shoot you in your manhood?"

Lang took a sip of his coffee and then started to roll a cigarette. "What's his name again?"

"Joaquin."

"Right. Jack in English. Well Rosa and Jack, do you figure to follow me all the way into the mountains and then to Wyoming?"

"If we have to," Rosa said.

"You don't even know if Grey Wolf is coming," Lang said.

"He will come," Rosa said. "For his son and to kill me."

"Because you're a witness to his many crimes?" Lang said.

"Yes, and because I helped the army capture him," Rosa said. "But they will not hold him. And then he will come."

"Finish up and let's get moving then," Lang said. "I'd like to find fresh water by dark."

Joaquin spoke to Lang in Apache.

Lang looked at Rosa.

"He said, what would you like for supper?"

Chapter Fifteen

Cox's deputy Alexander was having a cup of coffee in the way station cabin when Cox and Tweed returned.

Cox pulled Alexander aside to speak privately.

"Colonel West said the soldiers on the stage were his," Alexander said. "They were to guard the wife and son of Grey Wolf until they reached Fort Collins."

"Grey Wolf?" Cox said.

"Colonel West said Grey Wolf escaped when they were taking him to Fort Collins to stand trial," Alexander said.

"Escaped?" Cox said.

Alexander nodded.

"Grab a hot meal and then ride back to town," Cox said. "In the morning, load a month's worth of supplies on a mule and bring it to me here."

Alexander stared at Cox.

"I don't understand," Alexander said.

"I don't either, but I aim to find out," Cox said.

"We'll camp here and take that pass in the morning," Lang said and pointed to a notch in the mountains.

"How far is that?" Rosa asked.

"Ten, maybe twelve miles," Lang said.

"And after that?"

"It's a long way to Hole in the Wall," Lang said. "I'll need to find a horse."

"Where?"

"After the pass, there are some ranches scattered about. I can buy a horse and saddle hopefully."

"And us?"

"Do you have any money?"

"Some. Enough to buy a horse and saddle."

"Then we'll buy two, and you and the boy can ride to Fort Collins. Probably won't be more than a three-day ride due east, give or take."

"We will go with you to the Hole in the Wall," Rosa said.

"I don't think you understand what Hole in the Wall is exactly," Lang said.

Joaquin tugged on Rosa's arm and spoke in Apache.

"He wants you to go hunting for supper with him," Rosa said.

Lang looked at the boy.

"Go on. I'll build a fire," Rosa said.

Tweed and Cox sat in chairs on the porch of the cabin and drank coffee. It wasn't quite dark, but that twilight part of the day where it was caught in between the last bit of light and pending darkness.

"What did you mean before when you said it wasn't how Lang operates?" Tweed asked.

"Lang is a hustler, a con man type of outlaw if you will," Cox said. "He finds an easy target like a crooked gambler or cattle thief and targets them. I've never heard of him robbing a bank, train, or stagecoach before. And I've never known or heard of him killing a man in cold blood before."

"There's a first time for everything," Tweed said.

"That is true," Cox said. "But a man, good or bad, doesn't change his habits without a reason."

"I'm just a small-town sheriff, but I'm a good one," Tweed

said. "I've never concerned myself with the reasons why outlaws commit their crimes. I've always figured that's the job of the judge and jury."

"True words," Cox said.

Butler opened the cabin door and stepped onto the porch.

"The passengers want to know how long before they can move on?" he asked.

"Tomorrow morning," Cox said. "I'd wire your office to have some men come out, gather up the team, and take the abandoned coach back."

"Okay, Marshal," Butler said.

After Butler went back inside, Tweed said, "You're going after Lang, aren't you?"

Cox took a sip of coffee. "I'm going after somebody," he said.

Chapter Sixteen

Lang followed the boy across some gently sloping hills to a clearing of tall grass. Damned if a flock of wild turkeys wasn't wandering about the grass, pecking the ground as they aimlessly followed each other.

From a hundred feet away, Lang cocked the lever of the Winchester rifle as quietly as possible.

Joaquin placed his hand on Lang's elbow and shook his head no.

Lang lowered the Winchester.

Joaquin looked around for a rock, found one of throwing size, and picked it up. Holding the rock, he walked toward the turkeys from the left side of the flock. When he was about forty feet from them, they looked up and noticed him. Before the turkeys could react, Joaquin threw the rock with as much force as he could muster and struck a large male in the head. Without making a sound, the large male fell over dead to the ground.

As Joaquin raced to the fallen bird, the other turkeys scattered.

"Well I'll be damned," Lang said.

Alone at the corral, Cox watched Lang's black male. The horse was large, around seventy inches at the shoulder, and looked to be eighteen hundred pounds or so. A big horse for a big man, which Lang was, by all accounts.

Cox had a difficult time believing Lang had murdered seven

people in cold blood. Their paths had crossed several times throughout the years and in several instances, he had been close enough to speak to the man and look into his eyes.

Lang had the hard eyes of a seasoned war veteran who knew how to kill when necessary, but not frivolously. In all the reports Cox had read on the man's activities, he couldn't remember gunplay or killing even being mentioned.

Yet seven people were dead, and Lang was possibly afoot.

The question begged to be asked: why?

Cox looked at Lang's horse.

"Only one way to find out," he said aloud.

The turkey was delicious. The boy was resourceful, of that there was no doubt. But Lang was on the run from lawmen who probably believed he murdered seven people, and he couldn't afford to take the boy and his mother along to Hole in the Wall.

"Tomorrow, when we cross these hills and enter the pass to the valley, we will see signs of ranches," Lang said. "I'll try to buy a pair of horses."

"And then?" Rosa asked.

"We go our separate ways, I'm afraid," Lang said.

"I told you, Grey Wolf will . . ." Rosa said.

"You can make Fort Collins in five days," Lang said. "Even if he somehow managed to escape from the army, it will take him a lot longer than five days to find you."

"Then we will go to Hole in the Wall on our own," Rosa said.

"You'll never find it," Lang said.

"But you will, and we will find you."

"Do you even know what Hole in the Wall is?" Lang asked.

Rosa stared at Lang. The campfire reflected off her face, and she appeared quite beautiful in the pale, flickering light.

"It's sanctuary for outlaws, cutthroats, murderers, and horse thieves," Lang said. "It's a secret place where the worst of the worst can hide out from the law without worry. But, it ain't free. There's a cost to sanctuary."

"I told you, I have some money," Rosa said.

"The other thing is the only women allowed in the pass are whores," Lang said.

"Tell them I'm your whore."

"Traveling with an Apache son?" Lang said. "They'd kill me and make you a whore for real."

Rosa stared at Lang for many seconds. Her lips formed a thin, hard line. Her dark eyes narrowed to coal, black slits.

"I already am a whore," she snarled. "For Grey Wolf. I did not pick you to help us, but it's because of you that we need the help. Take us to Hole in the Wall, or so help me God, I will kill you in your sleep, you lazy bastard."

Lang looked at her face, saw that she meant it. He also realized that she was right; it was his fault that she was in this predicament.

"I'm going to sleep," Rosa said. "Tomorrow, see about getting us horses."

With that, Rosa marched to the campfire and curled up next to Joaquin.

Lang sat for a while, rolled and smoked a cigarette, and watched the stars. If he was lucky enough to reach Hole in the Wall, he had no idea who would be in attendance there. It was a very short list of outlaws who knew the secret location to the pass. Any one of them or none could be occupying the cabins when he arrived.

Doc Holliday was on that list, so was Sam Starr, the Younger boys, Jesse and Frank James, Kid Curry, Johnny Ringo, the Clantons, and a few others he couldn't name at the moment.

If he arrived empty-handed and the group in attendance was large enough, they might even kill him and the boy and abuse the woman until they had their fill of her.

He would need one hundred dollars to buy the supplies for the group to gain sanctuary. He'd used the pass three times before, and each time the price had gone up. He hoped it hadn't gone up again.

Lang finished the cigarette and then set out to gather additional wood to keep the fire going all night. Even though it was August, the cold mountain air chilled you at night, and it was best to sleep near a fire to avoid waking up stiff and sore.

He used the sack as a pillow and watched the stars for a while longer until he heard Rosa or the boy turn.

Lang looked over and it was Rosa who had turned. She looked at him with her coal black eyes.

"I know you must think that my son is just another half-breed dog in this world, but he really is not," Rosa said barely above a whisper. "I don't care what happens to me, but he deserves a chance to live a useful and long life."

Lang stared at her.

"You will help us," Rosa said, and she turned back around and hugged Joaquin.

Chapter Seventeen

Alexander arrived around noon with a pack mule loaded down with supplies.

"I see the stage has left," Alexander said when he dismounted.

"Right after breakfast," Cox said.

Butler came out of the cabin and stood on the porch. "Care for a hot meal, Deputy?" he said.

"The man can cook," Cox said. "Might as well stay."

"I'll put my horse in the corral," Alexander said.

Over lunch, Alexander gave Cox an update.

"Colonel West sent a runner to town this morning before I left," Alexander said. "He's sent out a patrol of sixty men to hunt down Grey Wolf and his band."

"Sixty or six hundred, they won't catch Grey Wolf," Cox said. "Not a second time."

"Grey Wolf is a savage, Colonel," Alexander said. "The army has trained men and scouts. You really think they won't catch him?"

"I know they won't," Cox said. "You mind the reports and the telegrams and if need be, send for Marshal Poule or one of the others. I'm leaving right after lunch."

When Lang opened his eyes a few minutes before dawn, Rosa was adding wood to the fire and Joaquin was gone.

"A man still asleep after dawn is a lazy man," Rosa said.

Lang sat up and listened to his back creak. "It isn't dawn yet, and where is the boy?"

"He went to gather eggs for breakfast," Rosa said. "He borrowed your hat."

"My hat?"

"Have some coffee. It's fresh."

Lang stood up, stretched out his back, and then grabbed a cup. Rosa lifted the pot out of the fire to fill it.

"What eggs?" Lang asked.

"We'll see when he returns."

Lang sat in front of the fire and rolled a cigarette. His pouch was half empty, and he had about forty rolling papers left. When the cigarette was formed, he used a twig from the fire to light it.

"I'm not a lazy man," Lang said.

"No?" Rosa said as she filled a second cup with coffee.

Lang looked at her.

"You steal rather than work for a living," Rosa said. "I call that lazy. What do you call it?"

From behind Rosa, Joaquin spoke in Apache. She turned and the boy held Lang's hat, which was full of brown and white eggs.

Lang stood up and looked at the eggs.

"Son of a . . . what are those, chicken eggs?" Lang asked.

Rosa spoke to Joaquin in Apache and the boy responded.

" 'Wild chickens,' he said. He found them about a mile east of here on some flatlands."

Joaquin set Lang's hat beside the fry pan.

"Do you have any more of that bacon left?" Rosa asked.

Chapter Eighteen

Cox arrived at the abandoned stagecoach and dismounted. He patted Lang's horse and then rubbed the mule's neck.

"Just sit still a minute," he told the animals.

Cox inspected the coach and scattered clothing more carefully. It struck him that the woman's clothes weren't really scattered haphazardly, but were strewn as if someone was looking for something and dumped the clothes to empty a satchel or bag. Question was, why?

He inspected the footprints in the dirt of the road. The woman was forced behind the other side of the coach and apparently violated three times, judging from the three different sets of boot prints.

The fourth man, possibly Lang, arrived later. There were no signs he'd violated the woman. Inside the coach, Cox found two sets of cut rope.

He stepped back and thought for a moment.

After the three men violated the woman they tied her up inside the coach, her and the small boy. Cox knew it was a boy by the size of the footprint he made in the dirt. Afterward, Lang arrived on foot and cut them loose.

"Why the hell were you on foot?" Cox said aloud. "And why was your horse a few miles away with the team?"

At the sound of his voice, Cox's horse neighed.

Cox walked to his horse and rubbed his neck.

"I'm just talking to myself, boy," he said.

Cox walked to the three sets of tracks that headed east. Lang, the woman, and the boy traveled together.

He knelt before the tracks to inspect them carefully. Tracks went north and the woman and boy followed. The woman and boy returned to the coach for some reason and then they set out north together.

"No, that's not right," he said aloud. "The man left first. The woman and boy stayed behind and then followed afterward."

Cox followed the tracks with his eyes and noticed something about a hundred feet away by a tall tree.

He walked to the tree and knelt before the remnants of a campfire.

"They stopped for lunch," he said aloud. "I'll be a son of a bitch."

By early afternoon, they reached the crest of the hills, and Lang decided to stop for a quick lunch and a brief rest.

Rosa built a fire and made some coffee. Lang decided to heat up the large can of beans and open the one-pound can of peaches for the noon meal as the dozen scrambled eggs with the last of the bacon they had for breakfast hadn't quite worn off yet.

"At the bottom of these hills is a valley caught in the middle of the Rockies," Lang said. "Good grazing land for horses and cattle. We should see some signs of a ranch once we hit the valley. If I'm lucky, we can find a rancher willing to sell us a few horses."

"How far is the Hole in the Wall?" Rosa asked.

"Four hundred miles as the crow flies," Lang said. "Without horses, we'd be in snow by the time we walked."

Joaquin spoke to Rosa in Apache and she answered him.

"What did he say?" Lang asked.

"He asked if you are a great warrior like his father," Rosa said.

"Tell him no."

Rosa spoke to Joaquin and the boy answered.

"He said, 'too bad.' He was just starting to like you," Rosa said.

Lang looked at the boy. Joaquin appeared to have a twinkle in his eyes. Lang grinned and then started to laugh.

Off the road, the trail was more difficult to follow, but not impossible. Cox had tracked many a man in his tenure as a marshal. Most tried to hide their tracks in dirt by using tree branches to scatter their prints. As tree branches don't get up and walk on their own, those were easy enough to follow.

Finding tracks over rocks wasn't as difficult as the untrained eye might think. A man on foot always disturbs just a little bit of the terrain. A few pebbles, a couple of rocks, a broken twig, but always something. A horse, on the other hand, disturbed a great deal and left tracks that were easy enough to follow, if you knew what to look for.

Streams were very easy to track a man in, especially shallow ones where the horse's tracks could be clearly seen in the mud below the surface of the water.

Open terrain of soft grass was the most difficult to track a man on foot across. Grass bends under a man's weight, but after a few days, the blades grow out and straighten up, and you have a hell of a time determining tracks. A horse made deeper impressions in grass that stayed much longer and were easier to find and follow.

But Lang was on foot.

Cox picked up the trail. Lang was now traveling northwest. The woman and boy were traveling with him.

Cox dismounted to inspect the marks left in the grass.

"Northwest to where?" he said aloud.

By five in the afternoon by the sun's placement in the sky, they reached the soft foothills and were close to flat ground.

"We have about two good hours of daylight left," Lang said. "We should find a place to make camp."

Rosa looked at the sky in the distance, at the dark clouds.

Lang had noticed the dark clouds hours ago, but didn't mention them. "It's dogging us, but it's still hours away. We need to find shelter or we'll have one wet night."

"Shelter where?" Rosa asked.

"We need to find some thick sagebrush," Lang said.

Rosa spoke to Joaquin and the boy nodded.

"I told him," Rosa said.

"Told him what?" Lang asked just as Joaquin took off running.

"That we'd follow him," Rosa said.

Lang and Rosa followed Joaquin for a good mile or more to an overgrown field of thick sagebrush.

"Look for the thickest patch you can find," Lang said.

Rosa told Joaquin and they split up and walked the thicket until Lang said, "This will do."

Lang removed his foot-long knife from the sheath and used it to cut an opening in the thick sagebrush. The thick wood of the stalks was difficult to cut through, but after a few minutes, Lang made an opening large enough to crawl into and move around.

He paused for a moment when the wind picked up considerably and the sky above darkened. The storm was just a few minutes away.

Lang got on his knees and cut through the thick brush until the opening was large enough for the three of them to squeeze into.

"Boy first, then you," he told Rosa.

Once Joaquin and Rosa were inside the opening, Lang gathered up all the cut stalks and branches and put them inside. He opened the cap of his canteen and stuck it in the ground so the opening would catch the rain. Then he entered, turned, and sat.

A few seconds later, the sky was as dark as night.

Lightning flashed and thunder boomed.

The sky opened and hard rain fell.

Within seconds, the flatlands of the valley were soaked. The winds blew hard and the rain came down on a slant, but inside the sagebrush, Lang, Rosa, and the boy stayed dry. The downpour lasted just fifteen or twenty minutes and ended just as quickly as it struck.

"The worst of it is over," Lang said. "We'll give it a few minutes."

Finally, the rain stopped and the sky lightened.

Lang crawled out first and gave his right hand to Rosa. Joaquin came out last and stood by her side.

"Let the ground soak up the rain before you bring out that dry brush and then build a fire," Lang said. "Me and young Jack here are going to get some supper."

Chapter Nineteen

Cox saw the storm blowing in fast from the south and dismounted to put his yellow slicker on. He knew the storm would strike and pass quickly, so he walked the horses and mule to the cover of a wide tree to wait it out.

He used leather strips to hobble all three animals as they spooked when lightning flashed and thunder boomed.

Cox had heard all the stories about lightning striking trees, but he also knew the odds were remote that it would strike the very tree he was standing under.

The sky went dark, lightning flashed, thunder boomed, and the rain fell in sheets.

Cox had to hold all three reins to keep the horses and mule from panicking as the water gathered and rose at their hooves.

The hard rain lasted fifteen minutes or so, then it lessened, the sky lightened, and the storm passed.

Cox released the reins and removed the leather strips.

"Well, that wasn't so bad," he said aloud.

He came out from under the tree and looked northwest where the storm was headed.

The rain would make following Lang's tracks close to impossible.

"Damn," he said.

The storm had the wildlife riled up and easy to find. Their choices to hunt were snowshoe hare or wild chickens.

"I think your ma would prefer hare as she saved the pelt from the last one," Lang said.

Joaquin looked at Lang.

"That's right, no English," Lang said.

Lang held his hands up to imitate the front paws of a hare and made little hopping movements.

Joaquin's eyes lit up in understanding.

"Lead the way," Lang said.

They walked several thousand yards, searching for signs of snowshoe hare until Joaquin stopped and pointed to a clump of thick brush.

Lang pointed. "There?"

Joaquin nodded.

Lang made a throwing motion. Joaquin nodded again, and then went to find some rocks. He returned with a handful and stood beside Lang.

Lang motioned to Joaquin and the boy threw a rock onto the brush. Several large hares scurried out and quickly hopped away.

Joaquin took aim with a rock, launched it at a brown hare, and struck it in the head. The hare fell over.

Three other hares raced away in a panic.

Lang drew his Colt revolver, cocked, fired, and, quick as you please, a large, white hare fell dead to the ground.

Lang slowly replaced the Colt into the holster.

Joaquin stared at Lang.

"Let's get our supper," Lang said.

Rosa used Lang's knife to expertly skin the two hares. Lang broke off more of the sagebrush stalks from inside the hole of their shelter to feed the fire.

Once the hares were skinned and dressed, Rosa fixed spits from the sagebrush stalks to roast the meat. She saved the pelts in her satchel.

The canteen had gathered a fair amount of rainwater so Lang filled the coffee pot with four cups and set it on the fire.

Rosa looked at Lang. "Perhaps you are not so useless after all," she said.

Joaquin spoke to Rosa in Apache and motioned with his finger as he spoke.

"He said, you are very fast with a gun," Rosa said.

"Right now, I'd rather be very fast with a horse," Lang said. "Let me have my knife and tell the boy to give me a hand."

While the hares cooked, Lang and Joaquin carved out an area inside the sagebrush large enough for the three of them to sleep in. Lang cut the stalks and Joaquin carried them out to Rosa.

When the hares were fully cooked, Rosa borrowed Lang's knife to slice the meat and load three tin plates.

"We need to cover a lot of ground tomorrow if we're to find a ranch and buy some horses," Lang said.

"How far to the mountains?" Rosa asked.

"I know they look close, but it's a few days' walk to the base," Lang said. "Clear across this valley."

"What about fresh water?" Rosa asked.

"We'll find a stream or pond in the morning," Lang said. "There's always something running down from the mountains."

Rosa spoke to Joaquin and the boy nodded.

"I told him to find fresh water in the morning," Rosa said.

"They trained him well, the Apaches," Lang said.

"He is the son of a chief," Rosa said.

Joaquin spoke to Rosa and then crawled into the large hole inside the sagebrush.

"He is tired and so am I," Rosa said.

She went to the opening, crawled inside, and lay down next to Joaquin.

Lang rolled a cigarette and lit it with a stick from the fire. There was a bit left in the coffee pot and he filled his cup. With the storm long past, the sky had cleared and the stars were out, as well as a half moon.

By the end of the next full moon, snow could be in the mountains. Hole in the Wall was the ideal place to sit out the winter and form a plan to deal with the law. But it was no place for a Mexican woman and her Apache son. That much was clear to him.

He felt for Rosa, her desperate plight and need to escape Apache slavery and to protect her son, but the cutthroats in the Hole in the Wall were even worse.

He remembered something he learned from his days in the war, a saying he'd heard. About having the devil you knew, or the one you didn't. It applied to Rosa's situation.

Grey Wolf was the devil she knew.

The outlaws at the Pass were the devil she didn't.

Lang wasn't sure which was worse.

He finished his coffee and crawled into the hole and rolled onto his side. The pale light from the moon filtered in just a bit, and he could see Rosa asleep, facing him. The boy had his arm draped over her waist.

Lang felt his eyes grow heavy and he drifted off to sleep.

A little while later, Lang opened his eyes and saw Rosa watching him from a few feet away, Joaquin's arm still around her waist.

"What?" Lang whispered.

"I was thinking how much better you would look if you shaved," she said and closed her eyes.

Chapter Twenty

Rawlins, Wyoming, was a one-horse town for sure, but it provided George, Hatfield, and Johnson some much needed time out of the saddle after days of back-breaking riding.

They spent the night at the brothel where each man paid five dollars for a woman and a bed. For an extra two bucks, a bottle of rye whiskey was provided.

Hungover and stinking of the whorehouse, they met for breakfast in the saloon.

"Believe I'll have me a shave and a bath," Hatfield said.

George looked at Johnson.

"Won't hurt us none either to clean up a bit," George said.

"We'll take us a bath, but then can we talk about divvying up the money?" Johnson said.

"Yeah, how about it, George?" Hatfield said.

"I ain't done my math figuring just yet," George said. "After we get cleaned up and buy supplies, I'll get a pencil and some paper and work it out."

"What do you figure it comes to three ways?" Johnson asked.

"More than four ways, boys," George said.

There was enough cooked hare left over from last night for Rosa to slice it thin and fry it in the pan with a bit of lard from Lang's supplies. Before dawn, Joaquin took Lang's hat, went to gather eggs, and returned with an even dozen.

Once the slices of hare were hot, she used the fry pan to

scramble the eggs, and they ate a hearty breakfast while the sun slowly rose and warmed the ground.

Joaquin spoke to Rosa. She nodded and said, "He wants to know if he should look for water."

"Yes," Lang said.

Rosa spoke to Joaquin and he nodded.

After breaking camp, Joaquin took the lead and traveled about five hundred yards in front of Lang and Rosa.

"The boy knows how to live Apache, that's for sure," Lang said. "But maybe you should teach him English if you expect to live in the white man's world."

"He speaks French and Spanish," Rosa said. "Besides Apache."

"That's great, except we ain't in France or Mexico," Lang said. "In America, English is the spoken language."

"Grey Wolf forbids learning or speaking English," Rosa said. "Even though he speaks English very well."

"Do what I say and not what I do," Lang said.

"What's that?" Rosa asked.

"The motto of a hypocrite."

"Is that what you think Grey Wolf is, a hypocrite?" Rosa asked.

"I only know him by reputation, but a man who does a thing and he forbids others from doing that very thing is, in my book, a hypocrite," Lang said.

"Your book? The book of a lazy man and thief," Rosa said.

"Who just happens to be saving your skinny ass and the boy," Lang said with annoyance.

"I don't have a skinny ass," Rosa said. "He's found water."

"What?" Lang said.

Rosa pointed to Joaquin, who was waving a stick at them from a good five hundred yards to the north.

"Come on," Rosa said and broke into a quick step.

When they reached Joaquin, he had removed his clothes and

was swimming in a large pond of fresh water.

"It's like a small lake in the middle of nowhere," Rosa said.

"Not quite," Lang said. "It's a man-made watering hole for emergency use."

"I don't understand," Rosa said.

"The local ranchers get together and dig out a large hole in the ground, and it gradually fills up from rain and snow until it forms a pond like this one," Lang said. "If there's a drought, they bring their horses and stock to the pond to water them so they don't die off waiting for rain."

"That means we are close to a ranch?" Rosa said.

"They build these ponds in a central location," Lang said. "Maybe two days' ride in every direction."

From the water, Joaquin shouted in Apache.

"He wants us to come in," Rosa said. "But I think you need a shave first."

"I don't have a razor, soap, or a mirror," Lang said.

Rosa opened her satchel and removed a razor and a bar of soap.

"Sit down. I will shave you," she said.

"You? I never had a woman . . ."

"If I wanted to cut your throat, I would have done so in your sleep by now," Rosa said. "Sit."

Lang removed his hat and sat on the soft dirt beside the pond.

Rosa went to the edge of the water and lathered up the bar of soap. Then she sat before Lang and gently lathered his beard.

Lang looked into her eyes as she opened the razor.

"You sure you know what you're doing?" he asked.

A coy smile crossed her lips. "Let's hope so," she said.

"Maybe this isn't . . ." Lang said just as Rosa placed the razor against his cheek.

"Hold still," Rosa said. "You'll bleed less."

"I don't want to bleed at all," Lang said.

And he didn't, as Rosa proved to be an expert with the razor. Within minutes, Lang was clean-shaven.

He rubbed his face. "Not bad at all. Where did you learn to shave a man like that?"

"I have many brothers," Rosa said. "I shaved them all and cut their hair. And an Apache removes all hair from his body, so I've kept in practice."

"How come you never mentioned your brothers before?" Lang said.

"There was no need to," Rosa said.

From the water, Joaquin shouted in Apache.

"He said to come in," Rosa said.

Lang looked at the boy.

"We should wash our clothes," Rosa said.

Lang looked at her.

"I've seen you naked before," she said and shrugged. "It's not that big of a deal."

Lang turned his back to Rosa and opened the buttons of his shirt. He slowly stripped naked and waded into the water. It was chilled from the rain, but not unbearably cold. He floated out to Joaquin and stood up. The water level was around five feet deep. The boy was gently moving his hands to keep himself afloat.

Joaquin shouted to Rosa, and when Lang turned around, she was standing naked on the shore of the pond. She was lathering her legs with the soap and gently scraping off the hair with the razor. If she was embarrassed at all about being naked in front of Lang or her son, it didn't show on her face.

"Good Lord," Lang said aloud.

Finished shaving, Rosa set the razor on top of her satchel, held onto the soap, and gracefully waded into the water.

She swam to Joaquin and Lang and spoke to Joaquin in

Apache. He took the soap and waded into shallow water.

"Your hair could use a good washing," Rosa said to Lang. "And as you've just seen, I don't have a skinny ass."

"Lady, if you don't beat all," Lang said.

"Are you a Christian?" Rosa asked.

"I was raised one," Lang said.

"They say in Christianity that cleanliness is next to godliness," Rosa said.

Behind them, Joaquin shouted. The boy held the bar of soap and tossed it to Lang.

"Your turn," Rosa said. "And don't forget to wash behind your ears."

Chapter Twenty-One

Cox spent the better part of the day trying to pick up Lang's tracks. He finally got lucky and stumbled upon their deserted campfire, which he estimated was five days old. He knew it was Lang from his prints in the soft dirt around the rocks assembled in a circle, although he didn't find prints of the woman and the boy at the camp. It appeared the woman and the boy were traveling behind Lang for some reason.

They were still moving northwest.

The woman and boy had to be slowing him down considerably if Lang was allowing them to follow him. That didn't make sense to Cox, that a man on the run from seven murders would take the time to help a woman and boy out in the middle of nowhere.

Cox used the deserted campsite to build a fire and then removed the goods from the mule. He fed the two horses and mule before seeing to his own needs, then made some coffee, baked beans, bacon, and tore off a hunk of cornbread wrapped in wax paper.

Cox ate before the fire. When he was done, he gave the horses and mule a good brushing. He gave each a treat of sugar cubes and then hobbled them.

Sitting before the fire with his coffee, Cox tried to work things out so they made sense to him.

The woman and boy had to be the wife and son of Grey Wolf. The soldiers were protecting her on the way to Fort

Collins. Lang and his men held up the stage at the way station for some reason.

What reason?

The stage wasn't carrying a large sum of money that he was aware of. Besides the woman and her son, there was nobody of consequence on the stage except for the old doctor, and he was far from a wealthy man.

There had to be a reason for Lang to hold up the stage.

There had to be a damned good reason to kill seven people in cold blood.

Cox sipped his coffee and then dug a cigar out of his saddlebags. He used a twig from the fire to light the end and puffed clouds of smoke as he continued to think.

Something went wrong.

Lang had a falling out with his men at the way station.

Over what?

Killing seven innocent people?

The three men spared the woman and boy, kept them on the stage with the idea in mind of violating her before leaving her and taking off. They also spared Lang, but took his horse.

Why did they spare Lang? They must have known Lang would go after them if they left him alive.

None of it made any sense.

And what was northwest that they were traveling that way?

Maybe Lang wanted to put some distance between him and his band of three?

Cox puffed on the cigar and mulled that thought around for a bit.

If Lang wanted to put distance between him and his three men, why drag a woman and boy across the countryside? They would surely slow him down.

Cox examined the situation.

The woman was the wife of renegade Apache war chief, Grey

Wolf. The boy was his son. Grey Wolf was captured by the army and on route to Fort Collins to stand trial for his crimes.

The woman and boy were being escorted to Fort Collins in all likelihood to give testimony against Grey Wolf.

Lang holds up the stage she's traveling on, things go wrong, and fate brings the woman, boy, and Lang together and on foot.

Grey Wolf escaped from the army and is on the loose again.

Cox took a sip of coffee and then thought, you're not running from the three men, are you, Lang?

You're helping the woman and boy.

"Son of a bitch," Cox said aloud.

Lang, Rosa, and Joaquin sat before a campfire wearing just their underwear. The heat from the fire was quickly drying them. They hung their clothes on sticks close to the fire to dry them out after they washed them with the bar of soap.

Earlier, while they were still in the water, Joaquin asked why there were no fish in the pond, but many bullfrogs. Lang told the boy through Rosa that the pond was made by man so there wouldn't be any fish, but the bullfrogs just sort of made it their home.

Damned if the boy didn't capture four giant bullfrogs for supper.

They ate just the legs, which Rosa cooked up with beans in the fry pan. While things cooked, Lang drank a cup of coffee and rolled a cigarette.

Rosa spoke to Joaquin in Apache, and he opened her satchel and dug out a pint bottle of whiskey. She added an ounce or so to the fry pan.

"For flavor," she said.

"What else you got in there?" Lang asked.

Rosa spoke to Joaquin. He opened the satchel again and produced a .32 caliber revolver and handed it to her.

"So you see, not only could I have cut your throat, but I could have shot you as well," Rosa said.

"Why you telling me now?" Lang asked.

"So that you know I won't," Rosa said.

She returned the revolver to the satchel.

"Would you like to sweeten your coffee?" Rosa asked Lang.

He held out his cup and she splashed some whiskey into it.

"Thank you," Lang said.

"Have you ever eaten bullfrog legs before?" Rosa asked.

"Can't say as I have."

"They are very good."

Joaquin spoke to Lang in Apache.

"Ah, God," Lang said. "English, boy. It's time you learned some English."

Joaquin looked at Lang.

Lang pointed to his chest and said, "Lang. Lang."

Joaquin stared at Lang.

Lang made a fist and thumped his chest. "Lang. Lang. Say it, boy."

"Yang," Joaquin said.

"No, not Yang," Lang said. "That's Chinese." He thumped his chest again. "Lang."

"Lang," Joaquin said.

"Yes, yes, Lang," Lang said, smiling. "I am Lang. Lang."

"Lang," Joaquin said.

"Yes, Lang," Lang said. He touched Joaquin's chest. "Jack. Jack."

Joaquin touched his chest. "Yack."

"No, not Yack," Lang said. "Yack is what women do when they get together over tea. Jack. Jack. Say it. Jack."

"Jack," Joaquin said.

"Yes, Jack," Lang said and thumped the boy's chest. "You are Jack. I am Lang."

"Jack," Joaquin said. He pointed to Lang. "Lang," he said.

"Damn straight," Lang said.

"Now that we know who is who, supper is ready," Rosa said.

Chapter Twenty-Two

Fully clothed, Lang and Rosa sat before the fire and watched the half moon shimmer off the pond waters.

Joaquin was asleep on the other side of the fire.

Lang filled his cup from the still warm coffee pot and emptied what was left into Rosa's cup. She added a splash of whiskey to each cup.

"I usually carry a bottle for cuts, bites, and bruises, but a sip against the night air won't hurt," she said.

"No, it will not," Lang said.

He rolled a cigarette and used a twig from the fire to light it. "I feel I should ask you something," he said. "How did you wind up married to Grey Wolf?"

"It is a long story," Rosa said.

"The night is young and we have nothing else to do," Lang said.

Rosa sipped her coffee and coughed slightly as the whiskey burned her throat.

"Go on, tell me," Lang said.

Rosa looked at him, and then her gaze fell upon the pond.

"I'm interested," Lang said. "Tell me."

"My parents were born in Texas when it was part of Mexico," she said. "After the war in thirty-six, when they were still children, their parents moved them to Mexico because they did not like Sam Houston. They came back to Texas when it became part of America in forty-five. I was born in forty-eight. They moved back to Mexico when the Civil War broke out in sixty-one. My father did not want his sons to die in a war that had no meaning for us."

"I know the feeling," Lang said. "Go on."

"We had a small farm across the Rio Grande," Rosa said. "Corn, wheat, a few cows, horses, and chickens. We were poor, but we made out all right. My brothers captured wild horses, broke them, and sold them to the Mexican Army for ten dollars a head. In sixty-four, when I was just sixteen, Grey Wolf and his renegades came across the border as they often did to raid. He was only twenty-one or -two at the time, but fierce and respected as a leader. He raided our farm. My father and brothers wanted to fight, but they were few against his many, and they had no choice but to surrender to save the women. When Grey Wolf saw me he decided that I was to be his. He told my father that as long as I was his wife, he would never return to the farm, but if I refused he would kill everyone except me and take me anyway."

"Jesus," Lang said. "So you went with him to save your family?"

"What would you have done?" Rosa asked.

Lang inhaled on the cigarette and then flicked it into the fire.

"Probably the same thing in your shoes," he said.

"He has other sons and daughters from other wives and women, but Joaquin is his heir to his leadership," Rosa said. "He will stop at nothing to get him back."

Lang turned to look at her.

"And if Grey Wolf gets his son back, he will make his son watch as he kills his mother," Rosa said.

"From Fort Collins to where we are is a hundred square miles," Lang said. "Even if he managed to escape, he would have no idea where we are or where to track us."

Rosa raised an eyebrow. "You think so?"

"He's that good?" Lang asked.

"Sometimes I think he is not human."

"Well, he still has to escape first," Lang said.

"Yes," Rosa said as if she knew he already had.

"You mentioned something before about how you betrayed him," Lang said.

"My job was to ride into town on a wagon and buy supplies whenever they ran low," Rosa said. "Grey Wolf, Joaquin, and me, we would leave the band and ride to town. I would ride alone the last mile or so. I rode into Colorado Springs and contacted the army at the outpost. I led them directly to Grey Wolf. Since he rode on the wagon, he had no horse and couldn't escape."

"Why?" Lang said. "I mean, why turn him in now after all these years?"

"Joaquin turns thirteen in a month," Rosa said. "He is then expected to kill his first white man to earn his place at Grey Wolf's side."

Lang looked at the sleeping boy.

"He's just a boy," Lang said.

"Not if Grey Wolf gets him back, he won't be," Rosa said.

"Maybe if you took him east to a big city or down to Mexico," Lang said.

"It wouldn't matter," Rosa said. "The only way to stop Grey Wolf is to kill him, and that is not so easy to do. Many have tried and died in the process."

Lang nodded.

"Tomorrow we'll see about some horses," Lang said. "Even Grey Wolf wouldn't be able to enter Hole in the Wall."

"Don't underestimate him. He is very resourceful and afraid of nothing," Rosa said. "He is as comfortable in mountains as on flat land. He doesn't care if it is summer or winter when his mind is made up to do a thing. The Hole in the Wall will not stop him if his mind is set on finding us."

"If we get snowed in there, he won't be able to get through the pass," Lang said.

"And neither will we to get out," Rosa said.

"He'll have to wait for spring, and a lot can happen between now and spring," Lang said.

Rosa looked at Lang. "Grey Wolf, when he decides to kill a man or raid a ranch or farm, he likes to do it on a full moon. The blood of his victims appears black on the ground. He calls it the silver moon. Most of his night attacks happen during the silver moon, and his victims never see or hear him coming."

"I've been thinking," Lang said. "If we can get some horses, we can make the pass well before the snow falls. On the other side of the pass is Riverton. That's a railroad town. I can put you on a train east or west, and you'd be clear across the country before Grey Wolf even knows what happened."

"East or west to where?" Rosa asked. "Who will allow a half-breed boy to live in a fancy city?"

"West to California," Lang said. "Half the population of California is Spanish and Mexican. The boys speaks Spanish, so he'll fit right in. San Diego is my guess."

"San Diego?" Rosa said.

"I've been there," Lang said. "It's a real Spanish town. You'll like it, and the boy could make friends easily enough. Even go to school and learn proper English."

Rosa looked out at the shimmering moonlight on the pond. "It sounds like a good plan," she said. "But first we must find horses."

"We'll find them," Lang said.

"I'm very tired," Rosa said. "I'm going to sleep."

While Rosa curled up next to Joaquin, Lang added more wood to the fire and then smoked another cigarette.

Lang was never a womanizer, even in his youth, although he

had his fair share of women over time. But never had he seen so handsome a woman as Rosa when she stood naked on the shore of the pond.

Lang finished the cigarette and settled in next to the fire. He closed his eyes and tried to sleep, but the image of Rosa invaded his mind and stirred feelings that had been buried so deeply inside him, he hardly recognized them for what they were.

Longing.

Chapter Twenty-Three

Cox drank the last bit of coffee watching the sunrise. Dawn was always his favorite part of the day. When that first hint of sunlight crested over the horizon, it was as if all the sins and evil of the previous day were washed away in the new light.

It wasn't true, of course, but Cox liked to think so nonetheless.

He fed the horses and mule and lingered over a final cup of coffee while they ate. Then he broke camp, packed the mule, and rode northwest, hoping to pick up Lang's trail by nightfall.

The heavy rain made it close to impossible to track anything, so Cox continued on the northwest path for most of the day. By late afternoon, he found a mountain stream and another campsite.

Three sets of tracks this time. Lang, the woman, and the boy. They camped together, ate fish, and left together in the morning.

Now there was no doubt in his mind that Lang was helping the woman and the boy.

Very peculiar behavior for an outlaw on the run.

Cox made camp before sundown, fed and watered the horses and mule, and then ate supper watching the mountains in the distance.

If Lang kept on a northwest path, he was walking directly into the Rocky Mountains.

What the hell for?

Cox estimated the distance to the mountains to be about seventy miles from where he was now. Between the stream and the mountains were days and days of foothills to cross.

By now, Lang was in the foothills, maybe on the other side headed to the mountains.

Two things came to mind.

Lang was meeting somebody at a specific place.

He was taking the woman and boy to a specific place or person.

It was still not making sense.

If they had horses, maybe it . . .

Cox paused to let his mind race for a moment and it came to him.

Lang was helping the woman and boy escape from Grey Wolf.

Lang was counting on Grey Wolf not being able to locate them as they made their way northwest to . . .

"To where?" Cox said aloud.

Just before sunrise, Joaquin stood over Lang, holding two bullfrogs, and said loudly, "Lang. Lang," in a singsong voice.

Lang opened his eyes to the smell of coffee. He sat up and looked at the boy.

"Is that breakfast?" he asked.

"Jack," Joaquin said.

"Close enough," Lang said as he stood up.

Rosa was at the campfire, scrambling eggs. "The frogs are for lunch. I will skin them and pack them in salt and cloth."

Lang grabbed a cup and filled it with coffee.

"What kind of eggs did the boy find?" he asked.

"Prairie chicken," Rosa said.

"He's a regular general store, that boy," Lang said.

"Come eat," Rosa said.

After breakfast, Rosa rinsed off the cookware in the pond,

then skinned and prepared the bullfrogs for transport and tucked them away in her satchel.

Lang rolled a cigarette and had a final cup of coffee.

"We'll continue northwest and should hit a ranch or at least grazing land inside of two days, maybe less," he said.

"What you said about taking the railroad west, it is a good idea," Rosa said.

"It is, but we'll never walk to Riverton," Lang said. "Riverton is near as far as the Hole in the Wall. No, we'll need horses."

"I've never bought a horse before," Rosa said. "How much does one cost?"

"If we find a kindly rancher, he might give us two saddled and shod for two hundred dollars."

"What about Joaquin? I have a hundred dollars."

"Okay then, but we'll cross that bridge when we come to it," Lang said. "Right now we need to get moving."

George entered the Greenly Saloon and found Hatfield and Johnson drinking rye whiskey at a table. He took a sip, filled an empty shot glass with rye, and swigged it down in one swallow.

"Got me a newspaper," George said.

"What's it say?" Hatfield asked.

"One story says how nobody knows why the stage was robbed and seven people killed," George said. "It also says how the wife of Grey Wolf and his son were on that stage. It says they think she and the boy survived, but disappeared. It says how she was on her way to Fort Collins to testify against Grey Wolf, who was captured by the army."

"Grey Wolf, captured?" Johnson said.

"It also says he escaped," George said.

"Don't that beat all," Hatfield said.

"There's another story says they don't know for sure, but they found Emmet Lang's horse near the abandoned stagecoach," George said.

Johnson and Hatfield looked at George.

"You dimwits, the both of you. Don't you see what that means?" George said.

"What does it mean, George?" Hatfield asked.

"Grey Wolf might be a murdering savage, but he ain't stupid," George said. "He'll get word it was Lang that held up the stage and he'll check things out. He'll blame Lang for what happened to his wife and go looking for him."

"Jeeze, I'd hate to have Grey Wolf tracking me," Hatfield said. "I heard he ain't human like the rest of us."

"Our troubles are over, boys," George said. "We'll let Grey Wolf do our dirty work for us."

"What will we do?" Hatfield said.

"We got thirteen thousand dollars each in our kick," George said. "I say we ride to Riverton and have us a time and then ride to Hole in the Wall for the winter. Maybe bring us some dance hall girls for those long winter nights."

"Sounds good, George," Johnson said. "What do we do come spring?"

"We'll worry about that in spring," George said. "Let's find us someplace to eat and spend the night. We'll ride to Riverton in the morning."

"Here is a good spot to noon," Lang said.

They'd covered about nine or ten miles since breakfast. The mountains, although they appeared large and looming, were still a good thirty miles or more away.

"There is some shade under that tree over there," Rosa said.

"Tell the boy I want him to come with me scouting for signs of a ranch," Lang said. "Tell him we're looking for a range that's been recently grazed upon."

Rosa spoke to Joaquin and the boy nodded.

"Lang," Joaquin said.

"Yeah, Lang," Lang said. "Let's go."

As Joaquin fell into step with Lang, he said, "Lang. Lang."

"I'm going to have to teach you more words, boy," Lang said.

Lang and Joaquin walked about a mile until Lang suddenly stopped. He pointed to a spot in the distance.

"See that low patch of grass there in the distance? That's grazed land," Lang said. "That means cattle. Understand cattle, boy?"

"Lang," Joaquin said.

"Yeah, right. Come on."

They walked to the range where cattle had grazed, and Lang knelt down and felt the grass. A month, maybe less, a rancher had his herd graze the site. The grass was slowly recovering.

Lang picked some blades of grass and showed them to Joaquin.

"Grass. Grass," Lang said.

Joaquin looked at the grass.

"Grass. Say it, boy," Lang said.

"Gas," Joaquin said.

"No, that's something you get from eating beans," Lang said. "Grass. Grr . . . ass. Grass. Say it."

"Grr . . . ass," Joaquin said.

"Close enough," Lang said. "Let's check things out."

Cattle make a large impact on their environment. They eat the grass down to the ground, and they leave tremendous amounts of waste behind. They carve a path as they travel that lasts for several months.

Lang estimated the herd grazed this range about a month ago. They came from the north and returned the same way.

"Looks like we found us a ranch," Lang said to Joaquin.

"Grr . . . ass. Lang," Joaquin said.

"Let's go tell your ma," Lang said.

"North maybe a day, day and a half walk from here we should find a ranch, maybe," Lang said. "Ranchers need supplies and a lot of them. They usually travel by wagon to and from a town. Wagons over time make a road. We'll separate by five hundred feet when we head north and look for wagon tracks. Tell the boy."

Rosa spoke to Joaquin in Apache and the boy nodded that he understood.

"I'll take the left, the boy takes the center. Yell out if you spot something," Lang said.

They walked for nearly five hours before Rosa called to Joaquin and Lang. She had found a road created over time by heavy wagon tracks.

"We'll make camp here," Lang said. "If we find a ranch tomorrow, I'll go in alone and speak with the owner. If all goes well, I'll bring you out to pick your horse."

"I'll make a fire," Rosa said. "You and Joaquin go see what you can find for supper."

Chapter Twenty-Four

Grey Wolf's forty renegades sat in a large circle around several campfires. Various things were on a dozen spits, cooking. Snowshoe hare, turkey, hens, and a few quail, although quail wasn't much of a meal. There were several loaves of bread the men munched on while they waited for the food to cook.

Although Grey Wolf sat in the circle with his men, it was clear who was in charge. While some of the men engaged in conversation, they spoke in almost a whisper, as if they were afraid to disturb him.

Grey Wolf smoked a pipe and read the newspaper some of his men got at a trading post that was friendly to Indians.

Grey Wolf read English as well as he spoke it. He read the story of the murdered people at the stagecoach way station, the escape of his wife and son, and the outlaw Emmet Lang.

Grey Wolf didn't understand the connection between his wife and Lang, but it was possible that Lang was aiding her and his son.

He'd never met Emmet Lang, but knew the outlaw by reputation. Lang was formidable as a foe. To kill him would be quite the prize.

They had whiskey from the trading post, but no one dared take a sip without Grey Wolf's permission.

Finished with the newspaper, Grey Wolf tossed it into the campfire closest to him. Tonight he would allow his men to get drunk and feast, for tomorrow he would send them south to

New Mexico Territory to conduct an errand and then wait for him.

Tomorrow, Grey Wolf would begin his search for the outlaw Emmet Lang. He would make his wife watch as he captured Lang and made his son kill the outlaw and become a man by taking his first scalp.

Then he would have his son watch as Grey Wolf killed his mother.

Grey Wolf, his heart elated and full, stood and announced to his men to break open their bottles of whiskey.

Lang and Joaquin caught three prairie chickens for supper. Or rather, Joaquin caught them by tossing rocks with precision-like accuracy. Rosa cooked the chickens with beans. After a hard day of walking, all three were famished.

They ate by the campfire and watched the sliver of moon crest above the mountains in the background.

Lang went through his pillowcase and found two cans of peaches. He decided they would share a can for dessert.

"If we get lucky and find a rancher willing to sell us horses, we can make Riverton in a week," Lang said. "I was thinking about this while we were walking this afternoon. We could sell the horses in Riverton. We won't get but half what we paid, but it will cover three railroad tickets and new sets of clothes for the trip west."

"Three railroad tickets?" Rosa said.

"It will take at least a week to reach San Diego on the train," Lang said. "If I have to hide out for the winter until I can figure this out, I'd rather do it in a warm climate. The Pacific Ocean is warm and as blue as the sky on a clear day."

"I have only seen the ocean once, and it was as a child," Rosa said. "It was cold and I was not so impressed."

"The Pacific is different," Lang said. "No snow, for one thing.

It's warm year round."

"It occurred to me that we need each other," Rosa said. "I need your help to get away from Grey Wolf and save my son. You need me because I can testify on your behalf that it was the other three men who killed those people and not you."

Lang looked at Rosa. Her face glowed in the light of the campfire, and he thought she looked not just beautiful, but radiant.

"You'd testify for me?" Lang asked.

"Provided you keep us alive," Rosa said with a hint of a grin. "Because I am of no use to you dead."

Cox sat against his saddle and watched the campfire while he smoked his pipe. The air was sweet with the smell of the burning tobacco. It reminded him of his wife, Johanna, and how she would always scold him for smelling up the house. During the warm months, he would have to sit on the porch to smoke. In winter, he would be restricted to his den and have to keep the door closed and a window open.

Cox felt sadness wash over him. He knew it came from thinking about his wife, which he tended to do often when he was alone. The only reason he kept working was to keep him from thinking of Johanna to the point it drove him insane with loneliness.

Life wasn't fair. Cox had known that since he was a child. But sometimes, life was downright cruel to a man. He spent his entire adult life as a lawman, chasing, arresting, shooting it out with, and sometimes killing, outlaws, and his wife was the one to die young.

She was just forty-four years old when she left him.

So he continued to do a job he had lost the taste for because he knew nothing else, and if he didn't, he would surely die of a broken heart.

Cox was startled when he felt wetness on his cheeks and realized it was tears.

Lang watched the stars and sliver of a moon overhead as he tried to sleep. The fire crackled, and tiny embers rose up and drifted away on a breeze. Bright one second, gone the next, like fireflies.

Like dreams.

He knew that he was just delaying the inevitable. He would be caught, tried, convicted, and probably hanged. But now that he'd started this game, he intended to finish it and see Rosa and the boy to safety.

Or go down fighting in the attempt.

It was true what she said, that he was the cause of her troubles. If he hadn't planned the stage job, she wouldn't be in their present situation. She would be in Fort Collins, under the protection of the army. Even with Grey Wolf on the loose, it was unlikely he would attack a fort full of trained soldiers.

The poets and wise men all say that in every life there is a turning point where you can't go back and must proceed forward no matter what the cost.

Lang knew he had reached such a point.

He turned and looked at Rosa. She was asleep on her side with one arm wrapped around Joaquin.

A split-second vision of Rosa asleep at his side with her arm wrapped around him flashed through his mind.

Lang blinked it away.

If he had reached that point, and he was sure he had, it was better to die caring for something than to swing at the end of a rope.

No matter what the outcome.

No matter what the cost.

Chapter Twenty-Five

"Do you hear something?" Lang asked.

They had been walking since dawn and it was now close to noon.

"Yes," Rosa said.

The road in front of them took a turn around a soft hill. The noise seemed to be coming from around the bend.

Lang held up his right hand and Rosa and the boy stopped.

The noise sounded like a hammer thumping against iron.

After a few seconds, the noise stopped and Lang heard a man mutter under his breath. Then the noise sounded again.

Lang glanced at Rosa.

"I'm going for a look," he whispered. "Take this and duck behind that tree over there and wait for me to return."

Lang handed Rosa the pillowcase and Winchester rifle.

He waited for them to walk to the tree well off the road, then he quietly ascended the soft hill close to the bend. When he reached the top, Lang got on his belly and looked below.

An old man was changing a busted wagon wheel, and from the looks of things, having a rough go of it. The wagon was empty. A team of two large mules was in the harness.

The old man was attempting to raise the wagon with a hand crank, but the weight of it was too much for him.

Lang turned and walked down to the road and waved to Rosa. She and Joaquin came over to him.

"It's an old man with a busted wagon," Lang said.

He removed his gun belt and handed it to Rosa.

"Stay out of sight until I call you," Lang said.

"Be careful," Rosa said.

Lang nodded, turned, and walked around the bend. He stopped about twenty feet from the wagon.

The old man was on his knees, banging the boxing metal insert that held the wagon wheel on the axle.

"Hello," Lang said loudly.

The old man looked up, dropped the hammer, and reached for a shotgun close at hand.

"No need for that scattergun, Mister," Lang said. "I'm unarmed."

"I'll say what my need is, and why are you unarmed?"

"To show you I mean you no harm," Lang said.

"What's your name?"

"Lang. Emmet Lang."

"Don't you pull the leg of an old man. It might cause my finger to accidently pull this trigger."

"I'm not . . . what do you mean pull your leg?"

"Got me a newspaper just two days old with some interesting stories about an outlaw called Emmet Lang. If that be you, you're a thief and a murderer."

"I'm him, but I'm not a murderer, and not really a thief in the common sense of the word," Lang said.

"What sense is that?"

"I held up the stage all right, but not to rob it," Lang said. "Just one passenger who stole money from the Indian tribes he was responsible for providing for. The men I was with took matters into their own hands. They double-crossed me, killed those people, and rode off with my horse. I've been on foot since."

The man slowly stood up and walked closer to Lang, keeping the shotgun aimed at Lang's belly.

"Why should I believe a word you say?"

"Who would say he's somebody he's not?" Lang said. "That newspaper say how the wife and son of Grey Wolf were on that stage and they disappeared without a trace?"

The old man looked at Lang.

"It does, doesn't it? Does it say how she was on the way to Fort Collins to testify against him to the army? Does it say how he escaped en route?"

"It does. What about it?"

"Grey Wolf will hunt her down and kill her for betraying him," Lang said. "That's why I'm helping her. Her and the boy. I feel partly responsible for their predicament."

The old man stared at Lang.

Lang turned his head. "Rosa, it's all right, you can come out now," he said loudly.

The old man looked past Lang as Rosa and Joaquin walked around the bend in the road and stood next to Lang.

"You Grey Wolf's wife?" the old man said.

"I am," Rosa said. "This is my son, Joaquin. Mr. Lang speaks the truth. I was traveling to Fort Collins to give testimony against my husband to the army. He did rob that man from the government who was a thief, but no one else. The other men struck Mr. Lang and left him after they . . . killed everybody. They kept me alive to rape me. Afterward, Mr. Lang found me, and he's been helping me and my son escape from Grey Wolf, who will kill me if he catches us."

The old man stared at Rosa.

"I have no reason to lie for Mr. Lang," she said.

"We need horses," Lang said. "We can pay for them if you have any to sell."

"How are you at fixing a wheel?"

"Fair. Have any supplies on that wagon?"

"Some."

"Rosa can fix lunch while we change out that wheel," Lang said.

The old man nodded. "My name is Daves. Jed Daves."

"Glad to know you, Mr. Daves," Lang said and extended his right hand.

Chapter Twenty-Six

It took about ninety minutes to change out the busted wheel. While Lang and Daves worked, Rosa cooked the two steaks the rancher had in his supplies, along with beans and two small hens Joaquin hunted. Daves also had fresh biscuits and half an apple pie.

"I got probably the smallest ranch here in the valley," Daves said while they ate. "My regular production is around three hundred head of cattle to market and a hundred horses or so to the army. My three boys are right keen in busting wild mustangs to go with the ones we raise. We'll never be what you call rich, but we make out all right."

"Did your wife bake this pie?" Rosa asked. "It's wonderful."

"My youngest boy, Kyle, baked it," Daves said. "My wife passed away four years ago from pneumonia, but she instructed him in the art of cooking, so at least one of her menfolk would be handy in the kitchen."

"I'm sorry about your wife," Rosa said.

"Me, too," Daves said.

"Can you help us?" Lang asked. "We need horses. I can pay for them."

"I can spare two, but you won't have to pay for them, just for the saddles," Daves said. "I've had my run-ins with the law in my time and even spent a year in a New Mexico hellhole for something I never did. You might say I respect the law, but I got little use for it. Say fifty dollars for the saddles, and we'll call it even."

"Appreciate it," Lang said.

"It usually takes me eight hours or so to reach the miserable excuse of a town they call Jacobs Notch for supplies," Daves said. "I'll be back this way around late afternoon or so tomorrow. Do you know what a line shack is?"

"Yes," Lang said.

"No," Rosa said.

"It's a cabin in the hills where cowboys stay during winter to keep an eye on things," Daves said. "Usually two cowboys to a cabin, but the big spreads sometimes use four. Around here, snow falls early and often and stays late, so the line shack is necessary to save any young cattle born in the spring from freezing to death over the winter. Mine is less than four miles from here. I'll ride you over and be back tomorrow, like I said, with some supplies for you. Day after that, I'll deliver the horses with one of my boys."

"We are in your debt, Mr. Daves," Rosa said.

"Make no never mind about that. I got no love for Grey Wolf," Daves said. "He killed my two oldest boys five years ago."

Daves read the look of shock on Rosa's face and said, "Weren't your doing. I'm sure you had no say in being Grey Wolf's wife. That you was testifying against him tells me that much."

"Your sons. What happened?" Rosa said.

"They were driving three hundred head to Denver to market," Daves said. "Grey Wolf and his band of forty ambushed my boys on the drive. Scalped both of them and stole the herd. The marshals and the army hunted him, but to no avail. Since then, I hire drovers to take the cattle to Denver and make sure they're armed to the teeth."

"I am so sorry," Rosa said.

"Not your doing, you or the boy," Daves said. "If you're ready, I'll ride you over to the shack."

"I picked here to build the line shack because this land is useless for cattle," Daves said as he rolled the wagon to a stop.

The land was made up of hills covered with dry brush and was unsuitable for much else besides the line shack.

A large corral stood empty in front of the two-room log cabin. To the right of the cabin was a toolshed and outhouse. Behind the cabin was a small barn.

"It don't look like much, but it will stand up to any winter, provided you rake off the roof," Daves said. "Come inside for a look."

Lang, Rosa, and Joaquin followed Daves to the porch. There Daves produced a key to the lock in the door from a secret spot under a porch railing.

He unlocked the door and opened it wide.

"Be a bit dusty with the windows shuttered, but it gets airy when they're opened," Daves said.

They entered, and Daves removed the wood plank from each of the four windows and opened the shutters. Light flooded into the cabin.

"Got two beds, table, and rocking chair," Daves said. "Good woodstove for cooking and stone fireplace. Pantry is stocked with canned goods, coffee, flour, sugar, salt and pepper, rice, beans, and lard. No fresh meat, though."

Daves turned to Rosa.

"I got time for a cup of coffee and a smoke if you care to make us a pot," he said. "The water pump is in the pantry beside the sink. It might take a few cranks to get her flowing."

Rosa spoke to Joaquin, and the boy nodded and then dashed out the door.

"Where's he going?" Daves asked.

"That boy is handier than a general store," Lang said.

"I figure every federal lawman is looking for you right about now," Daves said. "Local sheriffs, too."

"Not to mention the army," Lang said.

"That's right, the newspaper said about the two dead soldiers," Daves said.

"And Rosa and the boy, the army will want them back," Lang said. "But with Grey Wolf on the loose, I hesitate to try and deliver her."

They were in chairs on the porch, waiting for the coffee.

"Can't say as I blame her for wanting free of that murdering savage," Daves said. "When I deliver the horses, what do you figure on doing?"

"Ride north to Riverton and take the railroad west to California," Lang said. "The woman and boy could possibly settle in San Diego where Spanish is a prominent language. They should blend in right nice when the boy has a proper set of clothing."

"Be a good place for you to hole up while this mess gets sorted out," Daves said.

"It would."

The door opened and Rosa came out with two tin mugs of coffee. She gave one to Lang, the other to Daves.

"I am baking bread for tonight," she said. "Can I ask you to pick up some yeast when you go to town? Bread is better with yeast."

"I'll add it to the list and anything else you might want," Daves said.

Rosa nodded. "Thank you," she said and returned to the cabin.

"A pouch of tobacco and papers would be good," Lang said

as he rolled a cigarette.

Daves nodded. "By nature I'm a man who minds his own business, but I'd like to know about this man on the stage you robbed."

"Alfred J. Wallace, Indian agent for the reservations in Colorado," Lang said. "For years, he's been stealing from the tribes and pocketing the money. He was set to retire with forty thousand dollars in money that he stole from the government. He was the only one I planned to rob. Nobody else, and that's the gospel truth."

"Your men, what set them off like that to kill those folks?"

"I can't figure," Lang said. "Two were strangers, but one I've known for years. Name is George Bell. He did a stretch in Yuma, where he met the other two. Yuma must have turned him bad is all I can figure."

"Bad don't describe killing seven people in cold blood," Daves said. "Maybe he figured the money was all his and didn't want to split it?"

"I've thought of that."

"Why didn't he kill you?" Daves asked. "Seems strange he left you alive like that."

"Don't know," Lang said. "We rode together for a long time is all I can figure, but I'll be sure to ask him that very thing next time we meet."

"Best get to safety before you go thinking about revenge," Daves cautioned.

"I'm thinking about my neck being stretched, is what I'm thinking about," Lang said.

"I'm studying on something," Daves said. "What do you, the lady, and boy got in the way of clothes?"

"What's on my back," Lang said. "The rest was lost with my horse. Rosa left most of what she had at the stage."

"I'll see what I can do about that," Daves said.

"Mr. Daves, you've done enough," Lang said.

"Say you make it to Riverton," Daves said. "You're going to make a fine-looking bunch riding the railroad wearing rags for a week or more."

"I can pay you," Lang said.

"We'll talk about that when I return," Daves said. "Right now I best get going if I'm to make town before dark."

Lang walked with Daves to the wagon.

"By the way, there's wood needs splitting out back," Daves said. "You'll find axes in the shed. I'd appreciate it if you filled some of the woodbins behind the house."

"Sure thing," Lang said.

Daves climbed aboard the wagon. "Here comes the boy," he said.

Holding two hares and a chicken, Joaquin walked toward the cabin.

"Like I said, he's a regular general store," Lang said.

Chapter Twenty-Seven

Cox lost the trail shortly after breakfast and spent the better part of the day finding it again. Lang was still headed for the foothills of the mountains.

Cox knew the country somewhat, but where Lang was headed was anyone's guess. Maybe he knew a pass through the foothills through the mountains? There were many a valley in the Rockies where ranchers raised cattle and horses.

The sun was low in the sky when Cox stumbled upon the thick sagebrush where Lang, the woman, and boy spent the night after the last storm.

Cox dismounted and inspected the site. Lang had carved out a niche large enough for three in the thick brush to escape the torrential storm. Afterward, they made camp and spent the night.

Cox used the campsite to build a fire and cook some supper. While the beans and bacon and coffee cooked, he tended to the horses and mule. He ate before the fire and watched nightfall slowly settle in.

Afterward, he sipped coffee and smoked his pipe while he thought about Lang. In all his days as a lawman, never had Cox been involved in so strange a pursuit. Without the woman and boy, Lang probably would have found a horse somewhere and been out of the territory by now.

Instead, he chose to stay and help the woman and boy on foot.

Not the actions of a murderer and criminal.

Perplexing, to say the least.

If luck held out and Lang stayed afoot, he might catch up to him inside of a week or less. Cox hoped Lang would surrender peacefully and agree to return to make his statement on the matter.

With a gun, Lang was formidable, and Cox didn't relish a shootout with the man.

Spilling blood was the last thing Cox wanted.

He built up the fire to burn through the night, as the air had a chill to it from the higher elevation.

Cox turned in and thought about Lang for a bit more until sleep took him.

Chapter Twenty-Eight

Grey Wolf was determined not to sleep until he found their trail. If this outlaw Lang was aiding his wife in her escape, he relished the thought of taking the man's life. He relished the thought of killing Rosa and making a man of Joaquin by having the boy take the scalp of this outlaw Lang.

Grey Wolf rode through the day and into the night and into the day again. Neither he nor his massive horse seemed the least bit bothered by the lack of food or sleep.

Around noon by the placement of the sun in the sky, Grey Wolf finally dismounted by a shallow stream. He allowed his horse to rest, drink, and eat sweet grass.

While the horse grazed, Grey Wolf hunted two prairie chickens and roasted them on a spit. He ate them without cutting them up and afterward took a four-hour sleep.

He didn't dream.

Grey Wolf never dreamed.

When he awoke, he saddled the horse and continued riding.

The sun set, but he rode in the dark.

He traveled on instinct of direction.

He never tired.

He never wavered.

He rode until the sun came up and well into the late afternoon.

He thought of many things as he rode.

Thirty years ago, when he was still a boy, the white man arrived in large numbers. They built roads and passageways west to the lands they call California and Oregon. They made treaties with his people, then broke them and stole the land. The soldiers with their powerful weapons slaughtered his people, including his mother, father, and sisters. They drove his people off the land they'd harvested since before the white man even arrived. They killed all the bison and trapped all the game for furs for women to wear as hats back east. They stole minerals and metals from the ground to make their machinery and weapons. They put his people on reserved land where they nearly starved to death in winter. They lied, cheated, and stole and never once kept their word to his chiefs.

And while he grew from boy to man, Grey Wolf learned French from the fur trappers and English from the settlers and Christian missionaries. He learned Spanish from the Mexicans in Texas and New Mexico Territory.

When he reached manhood, Grey Wolf's sole purpose in life became revenge against the white man. To kill as many as possible and remove their seed from the land that rightfully belonged to Apache.

Grey Wolf rode through the night and into morning until he located the road traveled by the stagecoach.

He followed the road and found the location where the coach had been abandoned.

He dismounted and inspected the site.

There were many sets of tracks. One man went northwest on foot. Rosa and Joaquin appeared to follow him.

A week, maybe less, a man on horseback with two horses in tow arrived and then followed. Neither of the horses in tow had riders. One was loaded down with supplies. It was probably a mule.

This man was probably a lawman in pursuit of the outlaw Lang.

That would make a fine trophy for Grey Wolf when he caught up to the lawman. He would hang the lawman's scalp and badge on his saddle for all to see.

Grey Wolf led his horse to the abandoned campsite off the road where he assumed Lang had cooked a meal. Afterward, the footsteps still headed northwest.

Grey Wolf mounted his horse and followed the tracks.

Chapter Twenty-Nine

Shirtless, sweat dripping off his upper body and face, Lang slammed the heavy ax into a large piece of wood. It splintered into several smaller pieces.

Standing several feet away, Joaquin gathered up the shattered pieces and placed them into a woodbin.

Lang grabbed another large hunk of wood and placed it on the block.

Rosa watched from the kitchen window of the shack. There was warm flatbread on the table and hares roasting in the oven, which would be ready shortly. She sipped coffee sweetened with condensed milk from a can and watched Lang.

He was as tall and as heavily muscled as Grey Wolf, something she hadn't seen in a white man before. With each swing of the ax, the muscles in his back, shoulders, and arms bulged and flared.

She turned away from the window and checked the hares cooking in the oven. They were ready, and she removed them and set the large pan on the stovetop to cool.

She returned to the window.

"Supper is ready if you want to wash up," Rosa said.

Lang turned and looked at her.

"Couple more minutes to fill the bin," he said.

"It seems like a lifetime since I have had a meal at a table," Rosa said. "I would like to give thanks."

Lang looked at her as she bowed her head and said a prayer in Spanish.

Joaquin bowed his head along with her and recited the prayer, also in Spanish.

When finished, Rosa looked at Lang and then recited the same prayer in English. It was one he knew, the Lord's Prayer, and he said the words along with her, ending with Amen.

"You been teaching the boy Christian behind Grey Wolf's back?" Lang asked.

"Grey Wolf is gone sometimes months at a time from camp," Rosa said. "Teaching Joaquin various things passes the time."

Lang looked at the knife and fork beside his plate, then at Joaquin.

"Did you teach him about table manners?" Lang asked.

Joaquin had a huge chunk of hare and was about to rip into it with his teeth when Rosa scolded him in Apache.

Joaquin set the hare on his plate and picked up his knife and fork.

"Better," Rosa said.

As he sliced into his hare, Lang said, "I've been thinking about what Mr. Daves said about our clothes. He's right. We'll need to buy some new clothes in Riverton for the trip to California. A suit maybe for me, a new dress for you, and some decent clothes for the boy."

"I could use new shoes," Rosa said. "What I have are pretty worn out."

"We'll need maybe sixty or seventy dollars," Lang said. "I have more than enough."

"I have my own money," Rosa said.

"Then you can buy the train tickets," Lang said.

After dark, Grey Wolf finally decided to stop and rest for the night. He removed the saddle from his horse and brushed him thoroughly before allowing him to eat his fill of sweet grass.

He made a fire, although he didn't cook anything. He had a sack of supplies hanging off the saddle, and he ate a cold supper of biscuits, jerked beef, and cornbread that came from the general store where his men purchased the newspaper.

Afterward, Grey Wolf smoked his pipe and thought about Rosa and Joaquin.

He didn't mind killing Rosa. Grey Wolf had killed many wives in his time who'd deserved their fate. Some strayed while he was away and slept with his dog soldiers. He killed them and the guilty men. Others ran off, and he hunted them down and killed them and took their scalps to show the others what happened if you ran away.

Never had one of his wives run off with a son and betrayed him to the army.

That crime called for special treatment.

He would drive stakes into the ground and tie Rosa's hands and feet to the stakes and then remove all of her clothing. He would have Joaquin watch as he peeled her skin away from her flesh and then leave her alive for the coyotes and wolves to feast upon.

She would beg for death, but death would be slow in coming. Only when the coyotes and wolves ate through her stomach to her entrails and then her lungs and heart would life leave her body.

Before she died, Joaquin would be the one to end her existence. Grey Wolf would insist upon that. Joaquin would pass to manhood at his mother's expense, giving Grey Wolf his revenge in the process.

Grey Wolf fell asleep thinking of his revenge and the idea of his son, a man and warrior at his side.

Chapter Thirty

Lang rolled a cigarette as he sat on the porch with a cup of coffee. Through the open windows, he heard Rosa speak to Joaquin in Apache. A minute or so later, the door opened and she came out with a cup of her own and took the chair next to his.

"Joaquin has gone to bed," she said. "He wanted to sleep on the floor, but I told him the bed is large enough for the both of us."

"Has he ever slept in a bed before?"

"At the army outpost," Rosa said. "He didn't like it. He said it was too soft."

"He'll come to appreciate the finer points of a good bed once you get settled in California," Lang said.

"And what about you?" Rosa asked. "Where will you get settled?"

"I'm studying on that," Lang said.

Rosa sipped her coffee as she mulled something over in her mind. "I have a question I would like to ask," she said.

"Ask," Lang said.

"How did you become an outlaw, a man like you? You might be lazy, but you aren't stupid."

"It's a long, boring story," Lang said.

"The night is early and I'm not tired," Rosa said.

Lang tossed the spent cigarette and sipped his coffee. "I'm from Indiana, originally. South of a little town nobody ever heard of called Gates. It sits on the Kentucky border, and some folks said back then we stole it from them. My parents had close to a thousand acres of prime farmland they worked for thirty years without the help of a single slave, which is more than I can say about our neighbors across the river in Kentucky."

"What did you grow?"

"Wheat, mostly. Sometimes corn and potatoes."

"I can't see you behind a plow," Rosa said.

"It's hard work, especially in late spring and early summer."

"So what happened?"

"In sixty-one, before the war broke out, I was studying architecture in Boston," Lang said.

"Wait, you went to university?" Rosa said.

"You sound shocked," Lang said.

"It's just . . . I didn't think . . . never mind. Go on."

"I was just twenty at the time and in my second year, when the first shots of the war were fired," Lang said. "I left school and returned home to the farm. Soon after that I enlisted in the Union Army and was sent to New York for training. Because of my education, I was made a second lieutenant after training and served under Butler, Meade, Sherman, and Grant. By sixty-four I was a captain. I didn't get home again until sixty-six. I was discharged as a captain."

Rosa stared at Lang. Two lanterns suspended on the wall flickered their light off Lang's face.

"What aren't you telling me?" she asked.

"In the fall of sixty-four, before Sherman's March to the Sea, rebel troops realized their cause was lost," Lang said. "They formed vigilante groups and invaded Union states to enact their revenge. They looted, raped, and burned everything in their path."

Lang paused to roll a fresh cigarette.

"And?" Rosa asked.

Lang lit the cigarette with a wood match, inhaled, and then

said, "I was with Sherman on his march to the sea when I received word from a neighbor that sixty rebel soldiers rode across the border and burned our farm to the ground. They murdered my parents and kid sister, but not before they raped her first. Afterward, they hung them from this giant tree we had in the front yard. I used to climb and play on that tree when I was a kid. My neighbors said they gave them a Christian burial."

Rosa looked away for a moment to wipe a tear from her eyes, then she looked at Lang. "What did you do then?" she asked.

"When I returned home in early sixty-six, I wanted revenge against the men who murdered my family," Lang said. "But who were they, where were they, I didn't know. So I took an ax and cut down the tree they hung my family from and left the farm. I've never been back."

"I understand the loss of family better than anyone, but this doesn't explain the outlaw part," Rosa said.

"No, I guess it doesn't," Lang said.

"So, what does?"

"After I left the farm, I really had nowhere to go. I just sort of drifted," Lang said. "The south, mostly. I spent enough winters up north to last me a while. I rode through Kentucky, Tennessee, Georgia, Alabama, Mississippi, and Arkansas. Know what I saw a lot of? Fat-cat carpetbaggers. Know what a carpetbagger is?"

"No."

"Bankers and such that moved to the south after the war to help the freed slaves adjust and help with the reconstruction," Lang said. "They carried fancy luggage and bags that resembled fine carpet. What they did mostly was line their pockets with money they promised freed slaves and improvised business owners. They were nothing more than snake-oil salesmen selling potions. I watched a couple of them make a speech in the streets of Georgia and those men were so corrupt, I came up with the idea that if I robbed them, they would have no one to complain to. I relieved those two of almost three thousand dollars. That was in eighteen-sixty-seven dollars, before inflation devalued our money some."

"And?"

"And nothing," Lang said. "From there, I kept targeting carpetbaggers until they caught on and started using bodyguards. After that, I drifted west, and it wasn't too difficult to find corrupt men to target and relieve of their gains."

"None of them pressed charges?" Rosa asked.

"For them to do that, they would have had to admit they were corrupt," Lang said. "Like Alfred Wallace. If my plan stayed on course, who would he complain to? How could he swear out a warrant against me for stealing the money he stole from the government? The law figured out what I was doing, branded me an outlaw, but as long as nobody pressed charges, they couldn't do much."

"I understand what makes you do this, but I still think it's a lazy man's way to earn a living," Rosa said.

"Maybe so," Lang said. "But habits are hard-made and can be difficult to break. If I live through this, I will seek another, less dangerous, line of work."

Rosa allowed herself a tiny smile. "Have you thought about farming?"

"Not lately," Lang said. "I hated farming. Why do you think I studied architecture?"

"Were you any good at it?" Rosa asked. "The architecture?"

"Fair, but it was a long time ago and I'd have to start over," Lang said. "I'm too old to sit in a classroom with kids."

Rosa sipped her coffee. "Joaquin says you are fast with a gun," she said.

"I grew up hunting on the farm, but I never had much use for a handgun," Lang said. "The army taught me proper use of the Colt Model 1860 revolver. After the war, I taught myself speed through hundreds of hours of practice. I figured one day I might find myself in the position where speed was necessary."

"What's become of the farm?" Rosa asked.

"Cousins from Ohio took it over in sixty-seven," Lang said. "As far as I know, they still work it."

"Maybe when . . ." Rosa said.

The door opened and Joaquin stepped out to the porch. He spoke to Rosa in Apache.

"He doesn't like the bed," Rosa said. "He wants to sleep on the floor."

"Maybe we all should get some sleep," Lang said.

Rosa stood and put her arm around Joaquin. "Give me a minute to change and get into bed," she said.

After Rosa and Joaquin returned to the cabin, Lang rolled a fresh cigarette and finished his coffee.

It had been many years since he'd thought of the farm and his parents and kid sister, July. Her real name was Juliette, but early on he took to calling her July and the name stuck.

She was eleven when he went off to war.

Just fifteen when they murdered her.

The day he rode off to join the Union Army, she hugged him tightly around the neck and cried softly onto his chest. He told her it would be all right and that he would return before she knew it.

The last image Lang had of home before he rode off was of his parents and tiny July watching him ride off from the front porch.

For a long time, he believed he should have stayed on the farm and not joined the fight. He told himself that if he had stayed, his family would still be alive today. But that wasn't true. When the raiders came, they would just have killed him along with his family.

"Damn," Lang said aloud.

He finished his cigarette and coffee and decided it was time to turn in. Rosa had left the lantern on low flame on the table. He closed the door, extinguished the lantern, and wearily crawled into bed.

Chapter Thirty-One

Lang split a cord of wood and filled a woodbin before breakfast. It was the fifth bin he'd filled since yesterday. There were eight empty bins in the barn when he started. He wanted to fill all eight to repay Daves for his kindness.

With each split of a log, Joaquin gathered up the pieces and placed them into a bin. The boy seemed tireless and never complained, no matter what the chore. Lang could see the potential in the boy to be the warrior Grey Wolf wanted him to become. It was a question of who got to raise him and how.

If he grew up at Grey Wolf's side, Joaquin would become the savage, raider, and murderer his father wanted him to become.

If raised by Rosa in San Diego, there was no telling how far in life the boy would go, but savage murderer wasn't on her list of things she aimed to teach him.

Behind Lang, Rosa appeared in the open window. "Lunch is ready," she said.

Lang set the ax aside and looked at Joaquin.

"Food," Joaquin said.

"I see she's taught you a new word," Lang said. "That's right, food."

Rosa was plucking the two chickens Joaquin caught for supper when she heard a faint noise and looked up to see Mr. Daves approaching in his wagon. He was maybe a half mile down the road. She set the large pot aside and went around the side of the cabin to where Lang was chopping wood.

Shirtless, Lang's upper body glistened from sweat in the sunlight. She watched him for a moment before she cleared her throat and said, "Mr. Daves is back."

Lang set the ax aside and reached for his shirt.

"Let's take a breather, boy," he told Joaquin.

Although he didn't understand the words, Joaquin understood Lang's intent.

Daves sipped the fresh coffee Rosa served him at the kitchen table.

"Brought you enough supplies to last the trip to Riverton," he said. "And a fresh pouch of tobacco, papers, and a bottle of rye whiskey in case it gets cold on the trail."

"I'll be paying you for all this on top of the saddles," Lang said.

"We were just about to eat lunch," Rosa said. "Please join us."

"Be happy to," Daves said. "Breakfast in town isn't fit for a dog."

"Any word on things?" Lang asked.

"Ain't no real law in town, just a constable appointed by the county sheriff," Daves said. "But I did get a copy of the *Denver Star Ledger.* Says the Overland Stage Company has offered twenty-five-hundred in cash for information leading to your capture. And seeing as how that Wallace fellow worked for the government, another five-thousand-dollar reward offered by the government. I brought the paper for you to read."

Rosa looked at Lang, but he showed no reaction or emotion to the news.

"Any of the stories give my description?" he asked quietly.

"Come to think on it, no," Daves said.

"What about Rosa and the boy?" Lang asked.

"Just that they're still missing," Daves said. "Speculation on if they're traveling with you or on their own."

"Any mention of Grey Wolf?" Rosa asked.

"Just that he's being pursued by the army," Daves said.

"They won't capture him," Rosa said. "Not this time."

"I expect not," Daves said.

"I'll get the lunch," Rosa said. "I made rabbit stew from a hare my son captured just this morning."

Lang and Daves drank coffee from the porch after lunch.

Lang rolled a cigarette from the fresh pouch of tobacco and papers Daves bought in town.

"I'll be back around noon tomorrow with the horses," Daves said.

"We're obliged," Lang said. "More than I can say."

"I been studying on something," Daves said. "You could hole up at my ranch for the winter and by spring things should have calmed down enough to . . ."

"Grey Wolf would track us to your ranch," Lang said. "I can't allow that to happen. Our only chance, Rosa and the boy's only chance, is to stay ahead of him until I can get them on the railroad to safety."

Daves thought for a moment and then nodded.

"I expect you're right," he said.

"Well, I have another cord of wood to chop to fill all your bins," Lang said.

"I'll give you this much, Emmet Lang, you ain't a lazy man," Daves said.

Lang allowed himself to smile. "Just the way I make a living is," he said.

By late afternoon, the last bin was close to full. Lang chopped wood at a steady pace, and only when he paused to sip water from his canteen did he realize Joaquin was no longer stacking wood in the bin inside the barn.

"Jack?" Lang called. "Joaquin, where are you, boy?"

A moment later, carrying two buckets of boiling water, Joaquin appeared at Lang's side.

"Somebody taking a bath?" Lang asked.

He followed Joaquin into the barn where a round basin-type tub was set in the corner. Joaquin emptied the two buckets into the tub, which was almost half full.

Rosa appeared in the barn with two buckets of cold water and emptied them into the tub. "I can't stand being this dirty another moment," she said.

Lang looked at her.

"A bath wouldn't hurt you none, either," she said. "They way you've been sweating."

Lang shrugged. "Come on, boy, let's finish the wood."

Rosa spoke to Joaquin in Apache and the boy dashed off.

"I told him to bring me soap and a towel," she said.

"Right. I'll be outside. Chopping. I'll close the door," Lang said.

"Nobody is going to bite you," Rosa said. "Leave the barn door open or it will be too dark to see."

"Right," Lang said.

He returned to the chopping block and resumed chopping wood. Joaquin rushed past him with soap and a towel, and then took his position at Lang's side.

Lang split a log and Joaquin gathered the pieces and took them into the barn.

Lang could hear Rosa remove her clothing as she spoke to Joaquin.

Joaquin returned to Lang.

Lang set another log on the block.

The sound of splashing water sounded as Rosa entered the tub.

"Damn," he said and drove the ax into the log.

"Depending upon what time Mr. Daves arrives with the horses, we'll either get a late start tomorrow or first light the next day," Lang said.

"To Riverton is how long?" Rosa asked.

"Depends on the horse and what terrain we encounter," Lang said. "Eight days, maybe a week if we push hard."

They were at the kitchen table, drinking coffee after dinner.

"I know you said you were studying on where to go when we reach the railroad in Riverton, but I think you should go with us," Rosa said. "It would be difficult to spot you on the train wearing new clothes, and if we kept to ourselves, we . . ."

"The law, the army, by now they're looking for a man, woman, and boy," Lang said. "It's best we split up at the railroad. I'll ride on to Hole in the Wall and sit out the winter. Come spring, I figure things might have calmed down enough to contact the federal marshals and arrange for my surrender."

"Do you think that's best?" Rosa asked.

"If it saves you and the boy from Grey Wolf, I do," Lang said.

"What if I got in touch with the marshals in the spring and offered to testify on your behalf?" Rosa said. "I would swear in court you had nothing to do with the murders. What could they do to you then?"

"They could send me to Yuma for three years on a chain-gang, is what they could do," Lang said. "But that beats the end of a rope at least."

"Three years in a prison is a long time," Rosa said.

"Not as long a time as dead," Lang said.

"I suppose not."

Joaquin appeared from the side of the cabin and came onto

the porch. He spoke to Rosa in Apache.

"He said your bath is ready," Rosa said.

"My bath?"

"Take a lantern," Rosa said. "It's dark in the barn."

Chapter Thirty-Two

Cox made camp beside the pond where Lang, the woman, and the boy appeared to have spent the night. They had bullfrog for supper.

After he made a fire and put on some beans and bacon and coffee, he gave his horse a good brushing and grain. He didn't bother brushing the mule, just removed all the supplies and gave him grain.

While brushing Lang's horse, Cox noticed a chip in the left rear shoe. He always carried extra shoes and nails in his supplies for just such occasions. Tomorrow morning he would replace the shoe before leaving camp.

There wasn't much of a moon left in the sky, just a thin sliver. Its light reflected on the water in the pond, shimmering quietly as a soft breeze created gentle waves. Above his head, a million stars were visible.

Along with the night came the sound of the bullfrogs living in the pond. He ate with the constant croaks and twangs of the bullfrogs for music.

If it weren't for the fact that he was in pursuit of an outlaw, a woman, and her child, Cox might have said it was an enjoyable night.

That was what was missing from his life since his wife passed, more enjoyable nights. Nights of silent loneliness seemed more the normal now, and less and less tolerable as he grew older.

"Time to move on," Cox said aloud and was surprised to

hear his own voice.

When he was a much younger man just starting out as a lawman, the age of fifty seemed ancient, and the men of such an age still wearing a badge, an anachronism. Now he had become the very thing he'd once pitied, an old man doing a young man's job.

He remembered how he used to wonder why men his age still carried a badge. He now knew the answer. It was all he knew how to do in life. If you stopped doing it, what did you have left?

Cox read a newspaper story once about a prisoner in a prison in France. The man spent thirty years behind bars. When he was finally paroled, he immediately committed a crime so he would be returned to the only life that he knew, the life of an inmate.

The man had become institutionalized to a way of life and knew no other.

Being a lawman all your life was much the same thing.

Only your bars were the badge on your chest and the oath you took.

Maybe it wasn't too late for him to start over in life. He could take his pension, visit his daughters, and then maybe head west to California. He could use his pension to open a little store in a growing town and visit the ocean on days when he didn't feel like opening for business.

He could find another wife. A widow-woman around his own age, and they could settle down into a nice cottage and ride life into a comfortable old age together.

Why not?

Just as soon as he finished this business with Lang, he would put in for his papers and retire the badge he'd worn so faithfully all these decades.

★ ★ ★ ★ ★

Grey Wolf was going to ride through the night again, but around dusk the tracks led to a stream near the foothills. He stopped to inspect the campsite and tracks and didn't like the story they told him.

It appeared very much that they went fishing and took a bath in the stream. His wife showed no signs of trying to escape. Neither did his son.

Grey Wolf felt his blood begin to boil at the thought that his wife and son were taking aid from the outlaw.

The outlaw and Grey Wolf's wife would pay dearly for this unholy transgression.

Grey Wolf noted the lawman had also found the site and spent the night. He was no more than three days' ride ahead of him.

When he caught up to him, he would kill this lawman and take his scalp and valuables as a prize.

Grey Wolf doubted the lawman's mount was as good as his own, so he would set it free to roam the valley. There was little sense in killing good horses.

As he stuffed and lit his pipe, it occurred to Grey Wolf that this lawman was an excellent tracker and had been on point the entire time. Maybe he would have some fun at the lawman's expense. Track him until Lang was close, and then play a game with him.

Hunt the hunter, so to speak. See how far this lawman was willing to go in the name of his so-called white man's law.

Maybe he would allow the lawman to catch the outlaw and watch them do battle for his own amusement before killing the victor.

Grey Wolf set the pipe aside and rested his head against the saddle of his horse. Playing games with the lawman and outlaw would serve as amusement to pass the time, but he couldn't lose sight of his primary focus.

To murder his traitorous wife and bring his son to manhood.

Cox awoke in the middle of the night with an uneasy feeling in his gut. It was something tugging at him that he couldn't put his finger on, but he trusted his instincts, honed over the past twenty years.

He sat up and leaned against his saddle, pulled out his pocket watch, and held it up to the sliver of a moon. It was twenty past two in the morning, an ungodly hour.

Cox stuffed and lit his pipe, something he knew by habit that would return him to sleep before the bowl was finished.

He stood and checked the horses and mule and all were calm.

The woods and hills were deadly still, with not even a breeze.

If coyotes and wolves were about, they were equally as silent.

Cox stood beside his horse, watched him sleep, and felt the feeling that stirred him from his own sleep.

It was the uneasy feeling that he was being followed.

He hadn't seen one person on the trail since he left the stage line, but the feeling was there nonetheless, like an itch he couldn't scratch.

He could take a wide U-turn and backtrack and see if someone was actually dogging him, or he could up the pace and put more distance between them.

If there actually was somebody dogging him.

If he did backtrack and there wasn't, the gap between him and Lang would widen.

His first obligation was to the law, so he would continue pursuit of Lang and hope his itch was nothing more than an old lawman's imagination.

Chapter Thirty-Three

George, Hatfield, and Johnson soaked in hot tubs of soapy water at the Riverton Bath House. After hard days and nights of riding, they were tired and sore and in need of a warm bed, a full bottle of whiskey, and a playful whore.

"What do we do now?" Curly Johnson asked as he scrubbed his feet with a heavy bristle brush.

"Put on some clean clothes, have a steak at that hotel restaurant, buy a bottle, visit the sporting house, and hole up for a day or two," George said.

"I meant when we leave Riverton," Johnson said.

There was a bottle of rye whiskey on the floor beside George. He reached over the tub, grabbed the bottle, and pulled the cork.

George took a long, satisfying swallow and then passed the bottle to Hatfield.

"I been studying on things," George said. "I don't know if Emmet's been caught or killed, and either way is fine with me. We got thirteen thousand dollars each in our kick, and I think I'd like to stake myself to a claim in California where they mine for gold."

"Pan handling is hard work," Johnson said. "Might as well be a farmer."

"I ain't said you got to go," George said. "Neither of you. Just hear me out. We got enough money to last us a very long time, but I don't trust the law, and I don't know if Emmet is dead. I held back a thousand dollars from the take. We could pick up a wagon and load it with enough supplies to last until spring and wait out the winter at the Hole in the Wall. Maybe bring some saloon girls for the cold nights. Come spring, we go our separate ways, rich, fat, and happy."

"But why do we have to split up, George?" Johnson asked as he took the bottle from Hatfield.

"For one thing, you don't want to pan gold," George said. "For another, if the law is still after us come spring, they'll be looking for three men together, not three traveling alone."

"Well, me and Curly figure to stick together," Hatfield said. "We been together since Yuma."

"Suit yourself, but first we need to get to Hole in the Wall," George said. "Come spring, if you two want to stick together, I won't argue the point."

"How much you figure for the wagon and supplies?" Johnson asked.

"Maybe three hundred," George said.

"And the women?" Hatfield asked.

"Might be more," George said.

"Maybe we should get just one and divide up her time?" Johnson said.

"Long as they ain't no fights over her, I got no problem with that," George said.

"When do we leave?" Hatfield asked.

"Tomorrow we see about the wagon and supplies," George said.

Hatfield and Johnson sipped whiskey at a table in the Riverton Saloon while they waited for George to return from buying the supplies.

"What do you think?" Johnson asked.

"I think George plans to kill us when we reach Hole in the

Wall, that's what I think," Hatfield said.

"I got those same feelings myself," Johnson said as he tossed back his drink.

Hatfield nodded, gulped his drink, and then grabbed the bottle to fill the shot glasses.

"So what do we do about it?" Johnson asked.

"George is right in his thinking," Hatfield said. "Best place to hide a body no one will ever find is Hole in the Wall. We'll see to it, though, that the body is his."

"Kill George?" Johnson said.

"Before he kills us," Hatfield said.

"And we take his share equally between us?" Johnson said.

Hatfield gulped his drink and then lowered the glass.

"Of course," he said. "We're partners, aren't we?"

"I got no problem with that," Johnson said.

Chapter Thirty-Four

Lang spent the better part of the morning repairing broken fence posts in the corral. Joaquin stood by and helped with what he could, and Lang taught the boy new words as he worked.

Lang placed the boy's hand on a fence post. "Post. Post," Lang said.

Joaquin looked at the fence post.

"Say it, boy. Post," Lang said.

"Post," Joaquin said, shyly.

"Spit it out loud, boy," Lang said. "Post."

"Post," Joaquin said.

"Yes, post."

Lang grabbed a railing.

"Rail. Rail," Lang said.

Joaquin touched the railing.

"Rail," Joaquin said.

"Damn right," Lang said. "Rail."

Joaquin turned his head and looked at the road and pointed. Riding in a wagon with two horses in tow, Daves rode toward the cabin.

"I see him," Lang said. "That's Mr. Daves."

On the porch, watching Lang and Joaquin, Rosa said, "I'll put on a pot of coffee."

★ ★ ★ ★ ★

"That big suitcase has some clothes in it," Daves said. "Some from my wife's wardrobe that I never got around to cleaning out. Some for the boy from my youngest son. Some for you from my oldest son I couldn't part with, though they might be a tad small. There's some boot polish in a can."

Lang rubbed the two mares on the neck and glanced into the wagon at the saddles. "Mr. Daves, fifty dollars doesn't near cover all this," he said.

"The horses were sired in my range on their own. They cost me nothing. The clothing was just going to waste. Fifty dollars is more than a fair price for a pair of worn-out old saddles," Daves said.

"And the supplies?" Lang said. "They're at least fifty dollars."

"Would have cost me twice that and then some to fill my woodbins for the winter and repair the corral," Daves said. "Get the woman and boy to safety, that's all you owe me. And them."

Lang looked at the porch where Rosa and Joaquin quietly watched them from chairs.

"Stay for lunch?" Lang asked.

"That was a fine meal, ma'am," Daves said on the porch when it was time to leave.

"My son and I are deeply grateful for your kindness," Rosa said.

"Don't you sound like a schoolteacher," Daves said with a wink.

Lang walked with Daves to his wagon.

"Stay in the pass to Riverton," Daves said. "It might take an extra few days, but the chances of running across anything other than jackrabbits and mule deer are slim."

"I will, Mr. Daves," Lang said and extended his right hand.

"And thank you. For everything."

Lang found an old folding map of Colorado, Wyoming, and Idaho in a cabinet above the sink. By lantern, he and Rosa studied the map.

"Joaquin is asleep; would you like some more coffee?" Rosa asked.

"Yes, I would. Thank you," Lang said.

Rosa stood from the table to get the coffee pot from the hot woodstove and filled the two cups on the table. She replaced the pot and returned to her seat.

Lang had a pencil worn down to a nub and traced a route from their position at the line shack to Riverton in Wyoming.

"We need to stay off the roads and travel through the passes," Lang said. "We could make Riverton in eight days. We have supplies for twelve, and with Jack's skill at trapping small game, food won't be a problem. Water also is not a problem as many mountain streams run this time of year."

"I'm going to make corn dodgers for the trip," Rosa said. "Several hundred at least."

"That will take half the night," Lang said.

"Just a few hours," Rosa said. "There are cans of corn on the shelf. Can you open them for me?"

Lang sipped coffee and smoked a rolled cigarette from a chair on the front porch. The aroma of corn dodgers in the fry pan made its way through the open window and drifted by on a soft breeze.

The night was moonless, so the overhead sky was filled with more stars than he could ever count.

They were like twinkling pinpricks in a dark blanket.

It would be a week before the moon was visible in the night sky again, and that made traveling after dark nearly impossible.

And not just for them, for the law as well.

Rosa opened the door and stepped out to the porch. She held a cup and the bottle of bourbon whiskey Mr. Daves packed in the supplies.

"The last batch of corn dodgers are done," she said. "I thought I would sweeten your coffee, and mine."

Lang held out his cup and Rosa added about an ounce to it and about that to hers.

"Days are getting shorter, so we have to leave at first light," Lang said. "We need at least ten to twelve hours in the saddle to make Riverton in eight days."

"Do you think someone, the sheriff or marshal, might recognize you at the railroad station?" Rosa asked.

"Doubtful," Lang said. "Most towns, large or small, have the station on the outskirts and sometimes a short ride away from town altogether, so we'll ride directly to the station and buy our tickets. Once you're on the train, I'll continue north to Hole in the Wall. It's only another week's ride as the crow flies."

Rosa sipped from her cup and then looked away.

"You could change your mind and come with us?" she said.

"We've been over that already," Lang said. "The railroad police and US Marshals will be covering the trains. They might not spot us right away, but it's a long way to California. If I thought they could protect you and the boy, I might agree and take the chance."

"What do you mean?" Rosa asked.

"Nothing," Lang said. "Just a feeling I have."

"What kind of feeling?"

"That we're being dogged," Lang said. "Maybe not close, but nonetheless."

Rosa looked at Lang. "Grey Wolf can do that to a man when he comes for you," she said.

"All the more reason to get you on a train west," Lang said.

"Even Grey Wolf can't track a train."

Rosa nodded, stood up, and said, "I am very tired. I am going to bed."

Lang nodded and she went inside.

He rolled another cigarette and then sipped coffee. The bourbon went down harsh and stung his throat.

What he didn't tell Rosa was that he had a plan. After she was on the train, he would load up her horse with added supplies to weigh it down and ride to Hole in the Wall.

Grey Wolf would be tracking two horses, and without an alternative, would probably continue to do so right into the pass.

He would stay high in the cliffs and wait for Grey Wolf to arrive. If he rode in through the pass, Lang would know long before the Apache arrived.

And be ready for him.

If Grey Wolf rode, tracked, and acted like a white man.

Lang finished the cigarette and coffee and then went inside the cabin. Rosa had set the lantern on low and was asleep beside Joaquin in bed.

He blew out the low flame and then removed his boots and pants and crawled under the sheets of the second bed and closed his eyes.

The fatal flaw in his plan was simple enough.

Grey Wolf wasn't a white man.

Chapter Thirty-Five

The horses provided by Daves were of good stock. They rode them from sunup to noon without stopping once, and neither of them was winded.

They made camp under a tree for shade and rested the horses for one hour. Rosa made a pot of coffee, and they ate corn dodgers and divided up a large can of peaches packed in sweet syrup.

The horses ate tall, sweet grass that was abundant.

Lang and Rosa drank the coffee. Joaquin drank the thick syrup from the can of peaches.

Lang rolled a cigarette while Rosa rinsed the coffee pot with a few ounces of water.

"Now is the time to cover our tracks," Lang said.

He removed the folding shovel Daves packed in the supplies, walked fifty feet from the campsite, and dug a hole deep enough to bury the empty peaches can. He filled the hole and then covered it with some brush.

"We'll still travel northwest to Riverton, but from here on we stagger our routes to make our tracks more difficult to follow," Lang told Rosa when he returned to camp.

"That won't fool Grey Wolf," Rosa said.

"Maybe not, but if he has to take the time to look for our tracks, that's added time for us," Lang said. "Let's get rolling."

★ ★ ★ ★ ★

They rode hard until one hour before sunset and made camp near a shallow stream running down from the mountains.

"See if the boy can dig up a rabbit or a few wild birds for supper," Lang told Rosa. "I won't be long."

"Where are you going?" Rosa asked.

"Scout a trail for tomorrow."

Lang rode ahead for about an hour, searching for a path or gateway where their tracks would be more difficult to follow. The terrain offered little in the way of cover or protection from the elements or a tracker.

They would have to make it to Riverton on speed.

And hope that whoever was in pursuit, the law and/or Grey Wolf, was just a little bit slower.

Lang dismounted, tied the horse's reins to some low-hanging branches, sat, and rolled a cigarette.

He smoked, waiting for darkness.

Slowly, the sun sank below the mountains and darkness set in, bringing with it a slight chill to the air.

In the distance, he spotted the red dot of a flickering fire. In the hour-long ride, he'd traveled about six miles at a very moderate pace. The fire was easily seen from that distance, and probably twice that.

From all directions.

Lang finished the cigarette, grabbed the reins, mounted the horse, and followed the glowing dot back to Rosa and Joaquin.

A plump chicken was on a spit above the fire. Coffee was boiling in a pot. Beans with bacon cooked in the fry pan.

Lang dismounted and removed the saddle.

Joaquin proudly pointed to the chicken. Lang rubbed the boy's hair.

"Let's tend the horses," he said.

Although Joaquin didn't understand the words, he followed

Lang. When Lang removed two brushes from the well-worn saddlebags, the boy took one and immediately began to groom the horse he shared with his mother.

Tending the supper, Rosa looked at Lang as he brushed the horse.

"What did you see?" she asked quietly.

"Terrain made for an ambush," Lang said. "Probably clear to Riverton."

"We could find a road?" she said.

"Too risky," Lang said. "Too many people travel the roads."

Rosa turned the chicken on the spit, stood, and walked to Lang.

"When Apache is on a raid or running from soldiers, they never build a fire after dark," she said. "They camp before nightfall and wait for sunrise to build a fire and cook. I suggest that beginning tomorrow we do that very thing."

Lang held the brush on the horse's back for a moment and nodded.

"Tomorrow, change out of that skirt and put on a pair of pants from the young Daves boy," Lang said. "It's easier on the legs in pants than a skirt for hard riding."

"I still have my .32 revolver," she said. "But I can handle the Winchester."

"We only have the one, but if it comes down to it, I'll give you my Colt," Lang said. "After we eat, extinguish the fire and break out the blankets Mr. Daves gave us. There's a chill and they will keep you warm."

Rosa walked closer to Lang and placed her right hand on his shoulder.

"It's very strange, but I trust you," she said.

Lang looked at Joaquin. The boy stood motionless by his side and they made eye contact.

Silently, Joaquin nodded his head.

July came to him in a dream that moonless night. A little bit of a thing with big, owl eyes and soft golden hair, he loved his kid sister with all his heart.

Standing there on the porch with mom and dad, crying because her big brother was riding away to war.

He could see her face in his dream and it haunted him down to his very soul.

Over the years, he tried to imagine how she looked at fifteen, the age of her death. Had she grown straight and tall and blossomed into a young woman? Did she work the farm in his absence and have thick calluses on her hands? Did the young men from neighboring farms come courting to ask her to the spring dance in town?

Lang had no knowledge of that day the raiders came, but he could imagine the worst. Dad was pushing fifty at the time, but he was as strong a man as they came and would have put up a fight to the death.

Ma was a strong, fearless woman who would have protected July with her life.

And probably did.

By reputation, Lang knew the raiders murdered, burned, and raped the young women in the homes they invaded.

In his heart, he knew they had violated July before they murdered her and strung her up alongside his parents.

Lang bolted awake and sat up inside the blanket.

He was drenched in sweat, tossed the blanket, and stood up. The moonless night was dark, and he removed a wood match from his shirt pocket and lit it with the nail of his thumb.

Guided by the tiny flame, Lang picked up the canteen, took several swallows, and then sat beside his saddle to roll a cigarette.

The night was still. The horses were hobbled and asleep.

Rosa and the boy were quiet inside their blankets.

Lang smoked in silence and felt his body cool down from the chilly night air. Finished with the cigarette, he returned to his blanket and closed his eyes.

Rosa turned and wrapped her arm around him and brought her lips close to his face.

"We are all haunted by the nightmares of our past," she whispered.

Chapter Thirty-Six

The stream was the first one they came across in four days of hard riding. Lang decided to rest the horses for two hours and let them drink their fill. Rosa made a fire and put on a pot of coffee.

"Is there time for me to bathe in the stream?" Rosa asked.

"Go ahead," Lang said. "The horses need rest, and we've come far."

Rosa turned to Joaquin and asked him to try to find some eggs for lunch.

The boy nodded and looked at Lang.

"I need to keep watch and tend the horses," Lang said as he gave the boy his hat. "Understand?"

Rosa spoke to Joaquin, and he nodded and dashed away.

Lang removed the saddles from the horses and removed a brush from a saddlebag.

Rosa walked to the edge of the stream and stripped out of her pants, shirt, socks, underwear, and boots. If she was aware that Lang might or might not be watching her strip, she paid it no mind. When naked, she wadded right into the chilled mountain stream and dove under.

Lang kept his back to Rosa and concentrated on brushing the sweat and salt off the horses.

He was well aware of her womanhood, especially after she slept by his side the night he had the bad dream, but that was as far as it would go. They would part company in a few days and . . .

"Lang, it's okay to turn around now," Rosa called from the stream.

Lang turned, and Rosa was up to her neck in the stream.

"I thought you might like a bath," she said. "I won't peek."

Lang set the brush on the ground and walked to the stream. "I could use a bath. Turn around," he said.

The pickings were slim for eggs at the higher altitude. After about a quarter mile of walking, Joaquin found the nests of some prairie chickens, shooed them away, and gathered their eggs.

At the third nest, he didn't see the young prairie rattler sunning itself on a rock until it was too late.

Lang stood in chest-deep water that touched Rosa's chin. They were separated by less than three feet.

"That other night, what was your bad dream?" Rosa asked.

"My kid sister," Lang said. "I dreamt of her."

"And what did you dream?"

Rosa faced the shoreline and before Lang could respond, she screamed and rushed past him.

Lang turned and looked at Joaquin. The boy held his hat in his left hand and a dead prairie rattle in the right. Blood was dripping down from the meaty part of his right hand under the thumb.

Lang raced to shore and reached the boy just as Rosa grabbed his right hand.

Joaquin, covered in sweat, spoke to Rosa in Apache.

Lang grabbed the dead snake. "Prairie rattler. A young one."

"He says he was gathering eggs when the snake bit him," Rosa said. "He's angry at himself for not noticing the snake."

"Never mind that now," Lang said. "Get him to lie down over there in the shade and be still. The poison travels faster if you move around a lot."

Rosa led Joaquin to the tree and sat him down with his back to it.

Lang went to the campfire and added dry wood and brush to it, pulled out the knife from his holster, and stuck it in the fire.

"Get dressed," Lang said as he grabbed his clothing. "And then keep him as still as possible."

Rosa spoke to Joaquin in Apache, then went to her clothes and quickly put them on.

Pants and shirt on, Lang grabbed the coffee pot from the fire and set it aside for a moment. He turned to Rosa.

"That bottle of whiskey, we need it," he said.

Lang pulled out his bandanna from his pocket and set it on the grass. He removed the lid off the coffee pot and dumped the grounds onto the bandanna. Rosa gave him the whiskey bottle.

"Go stay with him," Lang said. "Keep him still."

Rosa went to Joaquin and spoke to him in Apache.

Lang poured several ounces of whiskey into the coffee grounds and wrapped the bandanna around them.

"Rosa, come take this," Lang said.

Rosa came to Lang and took the bandanna.

"Don't let any spill," Lang said.

He knelt before the fire and when the knife was hot enough, he pulled it out. Picking up the whiskey bottle, Lang walked to Rosa and Joaquin.

"Tell him I need to open the bite to drain the poison," Lang said. "That it will hurt, but I need him to be strong."

Rosa spoke to Joaquin in Apache and the boy nodded and replied.

"He says he will be strong," Rosa said. "He will not cry."

"Set the bandanna down and take hold of his arm for me," Lang said.

Rosa put the bandanna on the grass and took Joaquin's right hand.

Lang inspected the bite. The snake was young and the bite wasn't too deep, but Joaquin was a boy and the venom could be lethal to him.

Lang looked at Joaquin and nodded. Joaquin gritted his teeth and closed his eyes.

With the hot knife, Lang cut open the puncture holes of the snake bite. Joaquin bit down hard, winced in pain, but kept silent.

"Hold him tight. I have to go deeper," Lang said.

Rosa held Joaquin tightly about the shoulders. Lang pushed the blade deeper into Joaquin's flesh, twisted, and opened the wound.

Blood gushed.

Joaquin gasped in pain, but held his tongue.

"Brave boy," Lang said.

He took the bottle of whiskey and poured some into the flowing cut and picked up the bandanna and placed it against Joaquin's flesh.

"Tie it tightly," Lang said. "And keep him still. I'll be back directly."

"Where are you going?" Rosa asked.

"To find some tea," Lang said.

"Tea?" Rosa said.

Lang put on his gun belt and then walked away from camp and began inspecting the wildflowers. He covered several hundred yards before spotting the flowers he first was introduced to during the war by a company doctor.

Catnip, the doctor called it. Others called it the Hangman's Root because executioners ate its roots to get them into the mood to hang people. The plant seemed to grow wild everywhere, the doctor explained, and when tea was brewed from its leaves, it was used as a cure for many things.

The doctors gave large amounts of catnip tea to gunshot victims to lift their spirits, and whatever was in the leaves seemed to work.

Lang gathered up several large plants and ran back to camp.

Joaquin was against the tree with his eyes closed. The boy either fell asleep or passed out. Rosa sat next to him and held his left hand.

"Take the coffee pot to the creek, rinse it out and fill it with fresh water, and then stick it in the fire to boil," Lang said as he placed the catnip plants on the ground near the fire.

While Rosa went to the creek with the coffee pot, Lang removed the bandanna and inspected the wound. Joaquin's hand was swollen and red, but he expected that. The flesh wasn't hard, but soft, an indication that the infection hadn't settled into the hand.

At his touch, Joaquin opened his eyes and looked at Lang.

"You'll be fine, boy," Lang said.

Joaquin appeared to smile and then closed his eyes again.

Rosa placed the coffee pot in the fire and then stood next to Lang.

"He needs to sweat out the poison," Lang said. "Watch him while I make the tea."

Rosa sat beside Joaquin while Lang added some wood to the fire. When the water in the coffee pot boiled, he removed a dozen leaves from the catnip plants and rubbed them with his fingers to bring out the minty aroma and oils and then placed them into an empty cup and added boiling water.

From the pound bag of sugar, Lang added half a tablespoon to the cup and then half a tablespoon of whiskey.

He carried the cup with the spoon still in it to Rosa.

"When it cools enough, give him small sips of this," Lang said. "It will make him sweat. A lot."

Chapter Thirty-Seven

"It's getting dark," Rosa said.

She was sitting beside Joaquin next to the fire.

"I know," Lang said. "No choice but to keep the fire going all night. I don't think anyone is close enough to us to see it just yet. I think we'll be okay."

Rosa held a cup of the catnip tea and took a small sip.

"Where did you learn of this?" she asked.

"During the war from the army doctors," Lang said. "They use it for coughs, the flu, and to make a sick soldier sweat out a fever."

"It tastes pretty good and smells even better."

"Keep spooning it into him," Lang said. "I'm going to sleep awhile and then sit up with him during the night. This might take a few days."

"Are you hungry?" Rosa asked.

"I'll eat in a few hours when I wake up," Lang said.

Lang awoke to the aroma of beans and bacon cooking in the large fry pan. In the smaller pan, Rosa was scrambling the eggs Joaquin fetched earlier in the day.

He sat up and yawned.

"Hungry?" Rosa asked. "I thought it was a shame to waste the eggs."

"Starving. How is the boy?"

"Asleep. I didn't think it possible to sweat as much as he has, but it keeps coming," Rosa said.

Lang checked the stars in the sky. "It's around nine o'clock," he said. "I'll sit with him until morning."

"Then you better eat," Rosa said, and filled a tin plate with food.

Sometime during the night, Joaquin's fever worsened and he began to talk in his sleep.

Rosa awoke and sat beside Lang and her son.

"What's he saying?" Lang asked.

"He's talking about his father," Rosa said.

"About Grey Wolf?"

"He says that he is afraid of his father," Rosa said.

Lang looked at her. In the light of the fire, she appeared quite beautiful.

"And that he doesn't want to go back," Rosa said.

Lang looked at the boy. His face and body were drenched in sweat.

"His fever is too high," Lang said. "We have to get it down."

"How?"

"I saw this army doctor once treat a soldier with a fever from a bullet wound with ice," Lang said. "Stuck him in a tub full of ice until the fever broke."

"That's great, but I don't think we will have any ice for at least three months," Rosa said.

"This afternoon, remember how cold the creek was?" Lang said. "And that was with the sun on it."

Slowly, Rosa turned and looked past the campfire at the dark creek.

"Get his clothes off and then build up the fire so he doesn't freeze to death later on," Lang said.

While Rosa removed Joaquin's clothes, Lang stripped down to just his undershorts.

"Make a torch and hold it near the water so I can see," Lang said.

Rosa grabbed a thick log beside the fire, ripped off a piece of the skirt she had packed away in her satchel, and wrapped it around the log. She wet the material with a splash of whiskey and touched the fire. The torch ignited and she carried it to the creek.

Lang lifted Joaquin and carried him to the creek and waded into the water.

"Damn, this water's cold," Lang said. "Bring the torch closer so I can see him."

Rosa stood on the banks of the creek and watched as Lang dipped Joaquin into the cold water and held him there.

"How long in the water?" Rosa asked.

"That doctor I told you about kept the soldier in the ice until he started to shiver," Lang said.

Lang held Joaquin in the icy water until he felt his legs go numb and then carried the boy out and set him down for a few minutes and stood before the fire.

"I think it's working," Rosa said as she felt Joaquin's forehead.

"Just let me get some feeling in my legs and we'll go again," Lang said.

By the time Lang's legs went numb from a second trip into the creek, Joaquin's fever had broken. Lang carried the boy to the blanket in front of the fire.

"Wrap him up so he doesn't get a chill," Lang said.

Rosa wrapped Joaquin in a blanket as Lang warmed his legs before the fire.

"The fever is gone," Rosa said.

"How does his hand look?" Lang asked as he rubbed his legs.

"Better. Not so swollen."

"His body fought off the infection," Lang said.

"What about you?" Rosa asked.

Lang grabbed his pants. "I'd be lying if I said I was warm."

"There is no coffee, but the tea is hot," Rosa said.

Lang slipped on his shirt and took the cup from Rosa.

"Best get some sleep. Wrap yourself in a blanket and stay close to the boy to keep him warm," Lang said.

"What about you?"

"He won't be fit to travel for at least another day," Lang said. "I'll grab some sleep come daylight."

Wrapping herself in a blanket, Rosa looked at Lang. "You are a much more resourceful man than you let on," she said. "Why is that?"

"Have you ever played poker?" Lang asked.

"The card game? No."

"Well, when you play the game, the last thing you want to do is show your hand on the first go-round," Lang said.

Chapter Thirty-Eight

Lang slept until midafternoon and when he awoke and sat up, Rosa was adding wood to a campfire and Joaquin was sitting beside the hare that was on the spit.

Lang looked at the hare.

"Where did that come from?" he asked.

"My son is not the only one who knows how to catch a rabbit," Rosa said. "There is fresh coffee in the pot."

Lang grabbed the pot and a mug, filled it, and looked at Joaquin.

"His hand?" Lang said.

"Good. He can ride tomorrow," Rosa said.

Joaquin stood up and started talking to Lang in Apache.

"I told him what you did, and he says he is very grateful to you for saving his life," Rosa said.

Lang extended his right hand to Joaquin and the boy stared at it for a moment.

"Tell him this is how friends greet each other," Lang said.

Rosa spoke to Joaquin in Apache.

Joaquin extended his left hand and Lang took it.

"Damn right," Lang said.

George, Hatfield, and Johnson rode at a slow pace through the secret passage in the Big Horn Mountains to the Hole in the Wall hideout. George rode in a wagon loaded with supplies with his horse in tow behind the wagon.

Even though they were still a day's ride from the hideout and they failed to convince a whore from Riverton to make the trip with them, George was in fine spirits. They had beaten the law and Emmet Lang. They had a great deal of money and a comfortable place to stay the winter.

Johnson and Hatfield rode twenty or so yards ahead of the much slower wagon. Their spirits weren't as fine as George's.

"Still think George might be gunning for us?" Johnson said softly.

"Not sure," Hatfield said. "He bought enough supplies to last the three of us until spring. That could mean nothing, or he could be trying to lull us to sleep. Either way, I ain't giving him my back when we get there."

"Do you think George has somebody waiting for him there?" Johnson asked. "Maybe somebody he planned for before we pulled the job?"

"Could be," Hatfield said. "Just keep your eyes and ears open, and don't let your guard down around George for one second."

"Scouts!" George yelled from the wagon.

Hatfield and Johnson stopped their horses and scanned the cliffs above them. Two men with rifles took aim at them from a height of seven hundred feet.

"We can drill you where you sit, the three of you," one of the men yelled.

"Well, damn," George said. "Charlie Younger, is that you?"

In a clearing in the pass, Charlie Younger and a half-breed outlaw named Blue Duck met George, Hatfield, and Johnson.

"Boys, this here is Charlie Younger, uncle to Cole Younger and his brothers," George said. "I was sorry to hear about Cole, Charlie. That must have been quite a mess up there in Minnesota."

"Cole will be an old man before he gets out," Charlie Younger said. "This here is Blue Duck."

"That's quite a handle," George said. "Why they call you that?"

" 'Cause you whites can't pronounce Sha-con-gah," Blue Duck said.

"Sure enough true," George said.

"What brings you boys to the Pass?" Charlie asked.

"Gonna sit out the winter, me and my partners," George said. "Anybody else about?"

"Sam Starr and Maybelle Shirley," Charlie said.

"I heard of Sam Starr, but not no Maybelle Shirley," George said.

"She likes to be called Belle," Charlie said.

"How long you staying?" George asked.

"Pulling out tomorrow," Charlie said. "We been here a month and Belle is anxious to get back to Arkansas."

"Nobody else?" Hatfield asked.

"Not this time of year," Charlie said. "Nobody wants to get walled in when the snow flies, especially Belle."

Blue Duck looked at the wagon full of supplies. "You boys got enough to last till spring," he said. "How come you didn't bring a whore?"

"Couldn't get one to leave Riverton for the winter," George said.

"Well, come on boys, let's make tracks," Charlie said. "Maybe we can reach the hideout by nightfall."

Lang tossed wood on the campfire to ward off the chilled mountain night air.

"Mr. Daves knew what he was doing when he gave us these blankets," he said.

Rosa and Joaquin were huddled close to the fire with their blankets wrapped around their shoulders.

Lang pulled the coffee pot from the fire, filled a cup, and passed it to Rosa. Then he filled a second cup and sat beside her.

"How is his hand?" Lang asked.

"He'll be able to ride in the morning," Rosa said.

"We lost some time, but we'll make it up in the saddle," Lang said. "Any more of those corn dodgers?"

Rosa grinned. "Only about a hundred and fifty."

"Good," Lang said. "Because that's what we'll be eating for lunch in the saddle the next four days until we reach Riverton."

"Boys, this here is Sam Star and Belle Shirley," Charlie Younger said when Sam and Belle greeted them on the porch of a cabin.

"You ride all night?" Sam Starr asked.

George stepped down from the wagon and stretched his back. "Couldn't stand one more night sleeping on the ground," he said.

"We're pulling out first light, so you got your pick of cabins," Belle said.

"What you boys do you're holing up the winter?" Sam asked.

Johnson and Hatfield dismounted and tied their horses to a post.

"Who said we staying the winter?" Hatfield asked.

"Them supplies you got there in the wagon will last till April," Sam said.

"We got mixed up in a stage robbery that went bad," George said. "We lost our partner in the fuss."

Belle grinned at George. "That lost partner of yours wouldn't be named Emmet Lang, now would it?"

George, Hatfield, and Johnson stared at Belle.

"Me and Sam rode north to Cody for a few days and I picked up a copy of the *Cheyenne Ledger*," Belle said. "Seems an outlaw named Emmet Lang is still missing, along with the wife and son of Grey Wolf. Seems Grey Wolf and his pack are on the warpath."

"We got nothing to do with Grey Wolf and his bunch," George said.

"For your sake, I hope not," Blue Duck said. "Even I got the good sense not to mess with that savage."

"The newspaper story said how Grey Wolf won't stop his raids until Lang is dead and his wife and son are returned," Belle said.

"What raids?" George asked.

"It didn't say specifically," Belle said.

"Well, like I said, we got nothing to do with no Grey Wolf," George said.

"Let's hope he sees it the same way," Belle said.

"Come on, boys, let's get the supplies loaded into a cabin," George said.

Chapter Thirty-Nine

Grey Wolf rode into the abandoned campsite at the pond close to dusk and inspected the area carefully.

The outlaw and Grey Wolf's wife and son spent the night here maybe five or six nights ago. Joaquin caught bullfrogs for supper the way he taught the boy when he was much younger. They took a bath and washed their clothes and then rode out in the morning.

The lawman rode through just yesterday. He made camp, spent the night, and left in the morning.

Grey Wolf led his horse to the pond to allow him to drink and filled his canteen with fresh water.

It was too late to catch bullfrogs, so he ate a cold supper of hard biscuits and jerked beef from his sack of supplies. He would catch a few bullfrogs for breakfast and cook them on a fire, but tonight he would settle for cold food and his pipe.

Grey Wolf sat against the saddle, smoked his pipe, and watched the stars as night fell around him.

Bullfrogs croaked in the pond.

A slight breeze blew from the north.

Grey Wolf noticed the red dot on the horizon and stared at it in disbelief.

The lawman had made a campfire.

He was no more than ten miles to the north.

Grey Wolf put out the pipe, stood, and saddled his horse.

He rode hard for thirty minutes and dismounted about three

hundred yards from the campfire.

The fire was large, much too large for cooking a meal and to keep warm.

There was no smell of food cooking on the breeze.

Grey Wolf removed his Winchester rifle from the saddle, cocked the lever, and walked his horse to the blazing bonfire.

When he reached the fire, he released the horse and held the rifle high in the air and stood in front of the tall flames.

The horse whinnied and snorted nervously at the crackling flames.

Grey Wolf beat his chest defiantly with the Winchester.

"Lawman . . . ?" he shouted. "Do you see what you came to see?"

Grey Wolf lowered the Winchester to his side and scanned the darkness.

"I'm right here, Lawman," he shouted. "Take your best shot. You won't get another, I promise you."

Grey Wolf waited in front of the fire, but no response was forthcoming.

He spat on the ground in disgust.

"Coward," he said.

Five hundred yards to the west, Cox stood beside his horse and used the saddle as a resting post to steady his high-power army binoculars. With the bonfire illuminating Grey Wolf, Cox could clearly see the Apache Indian.

He beat his chest with his rifle and screamed his challenge into the night.

After a while, Grey Wolf settled down and made camp near the fire.

Cox lowered the binoculars and put them into his saddlebags.

Come morning, Grey Wolf would have a difficult time picking up his tracks as he removed his boots and walked barefoot to the site where he built the fire. When he returned to the hobbled horses, he made a wide U-turn and came up to them from the south.

Come daybreak, would Grey Wolf lose a half day tracking him, or continue northeast after Lang and his wife and son?

Cox mounted his horse, and with Lang's horse and the mule in tow, rode south for about a mile and set up a cold camp.

Grey Wolf smoked his pipe in front of the slowly dwindling bonfire to help soothe his still seething anger.

This lawman was smarter and more resilient than he'd anticipated.

That would make the lawman a much bigger prize when he killed him and took his scalp.

Chapter Forty

Close to midnight, George, Johnson, and Hatfield sat on the porch of a large cabin and shared whiskey with Sam Starr, Belle Shirley, Charlie Younger, and Blue Duck.

"Who is this Emmet Lang?" Blue Duck asked.

Belle picked up the whiskey bottle from the porch and filled everyone's shot glass.

"I've heard the name, but I never had the pleasure," she said.

"I met him a few times over the years," Charlie Younger said. "He plays it close to the vest. Don't talk much and don't show off none how good with a gun he is."

"And how good would that be?" Blue Duck asked.

George tossed back his shot and looked at Blue Duck. "As good as Holliday, Earp, and Hickok," he said. "I seen him draw down on two lawmen one time. Neither cleared their holster."

"He kill them?" Sam asked.

"Naw," George said. "Damndest thing I ever saw. He made them take off all their clothes and walk away in shame."

"All their . . . If that don't beat all," Sam said.

"The newspaper said he's running from the law and the army," Belle said. "He's suspected of killing a bunch of people and kidnapping the wife of Grey Wolf. That doesn't sound like a man who spared the lives of two law dogs."

"Don't matter now, does it?" George said. "Lang ain't escaping the law this time, and if the law don't get him, Grey Wolf will."

"Well, we can debate this all night, but I'm going to bed," Belle said. "We leave at first light for Arkansas and it's a long way off."

Walking to their cabin, Blue Duck said to Charlie Younger, "What do you think about that?"

"Killing people ain't Lang's way," Charlie said. "I seen him back away from many a fight 'cause it didn't make no good sense to him to shed blood, but if you back him into a corner, he's deadlier than a diamondback rattler."

"So them three got a problem?" Blue Duck said.

Charlie nodded. "Seems to me, they plan to hole up here until that problem goes away."

"Will it?"

"Not likely," Charlie said.

"Then it's good we won't be around," Blue Duck said.

Chapter Forty-One

Grey Wolf decided not to waste time hunting down the lawman. His time was better spent tracking the outlaw and his wife and son. The lawman would be around, either a day ahead or behind him, and Grey Wolf would deal with him when the need arose.

It was doubtful the lawman could keep pace with Grey Wolf, especially loaded down with a second horse and mule, so he wasn't worried the lawman would get the jump on him.

The bonfire was a test of a hunch, and now that the hunch became real, the lawman would keep his distance.

After a cold breakfast and some water, Grey Wolf mounted his horse and rode nonstop until dark. He started to recognize the territory. Soon he would be in the cattle country of the white ranchers. If they continued on this route, it would take them north into Wyoming.

That was good.

Wyoming was good land and open country, an excellent place to die.

Grey Wolf was in such a good mood that he hunted a large hare, built a campfire, and ate a good meal with total disregard for the lawman.

"He did well today," Lang said. "We covered a lot of ground. Tell him that."

Joaquin was brushing the horses while Lang and Rosa built a fire to cook the two hens the boy caught on the ride.

Rosa spoke to Joaquin in Apache and the boy responded.

"He said that his hand is better and tomorrow we can cover even more ground," Rosa said.

"We'll have to if we're to make Riverton in the next three days," Lang said.

Stirring the fire with a stick, Rosa looked at Lang.

"The moon is up tonight," Lang said. "It will be full inside a week, and we don't want to get caught out here under a full moon."

Rosa nodded.

"I wish you'd reconsider coming with us to California," Rosa said.

"I'm tired, Rosa," Lang said. "Of the running, of the life I've led. I'm tired of being a lazy man. My only chance at fixing that is to surrender to the law and serve my time. I figure three years isn't such a long time if the law believes your written testimony to the court."

Rosa nodded. "I best fix the hens before it gets dark," she said.

"I'll give the boy a hand with the horses," Lang said.

It bothered him to lie to Rosa about his plan to lead Grey Wolf into the Hole in the Wall pass, but he had little choice in the matter.

Rosa and the boy had come to mean a great deal to him, and he would be damned if he would allow Grey Wolf to capture and murder her and raise the boy to manhood.

He dug out a second brush from a saddlebag and stood beside Joaquin.

The boy smiled at him as Lang started to brush the other horse.

After eating the hare, Grey Wolf broke out the bottle of rye whiskey he kept in his saddlebags.

He sipped slowly as he smoked his pipe before the fire.

No man, white or red, had the right to steal another man's wife and son.

As he sipped whiskey, Grey Wolf felt his skin flush as his temper grew from thinking about Rosa.

It was obvious that she was not a captive and chose to be with this outlaw Lang. That in itself was an offense punishable by death, but her offense was even worse than that.

She betrayed the oath she pledged to her family that she would not run away in order to spare their lives.

Once the business of killing the outlaw, Rosa, and the lawman was done, Grey Wolf would reunite with his dog soldiers, and they would ride to Mexico and wipe out all living seed of Rosa's family.

Joaquin would use a tomahawk and before the raid was over, it would be stained with blood.

Her son would take his rightful place at Grey Wolf's right hand, and Rosa would be reduced to nothing more than a faded memory.

Grey Wolf looked up at the sliver of the new moon.

And like the alpha male of his namesake, he howled long and loud.

Lang rolled a cigarette and smoked in front of the dwindling campfire. Rosa sat next to him. Each had a blanket around their shoulders.

"Mr. Daves gave us four blankets," Lang said. "You and the boy best take the extra one tonight. Once the fire goes out, it's going to get chilly."

"The three of us can share it," Rosa said.

Lang looked at her. The sliver of moon cast her face in pale light that made her skin glow like fresh cream.

"Come on, we need to get up early," Rosa said.

She stood up and walked to Joaquin, who was already asleep. She got down next to Joaquin, facing away from him and covered herself with the blanket.

Lang tossed the cigarette into the dwindling fire, stood, and picked up the remaining two blankets. He covered Rosa and Joaquin with the extra blanket, and then got down next to Rosa, facing away from her, and tossed the blanket over himself.

Rosa extended her arm to hug Lang around his chest.

And for a brief moment in time, nothing else mattered.

CHAPTER FORTY-TWO

The northwest ride to Riverton cut across the railroad tracks from the east. Lang dismounted to give his horse a brief rest.

He rolled a cigarette while the horse ate some sweet grass.

In the distance, some thirty miles to the west, the Big Horn Mountains dominated the scenery. Beyond that, another twenty miles through the mountains was the way to the secret location to the Hole in the Wall hideout.

Riverton was just four hours to the north.

An hour or so to the south, Rosa and Joaquin were setting up camp for a late afternoon lunch.

Lang finished the cigarette, mounted the horse, and rode south to Rosa and the boy.

Two prairie hens were roasting on sticks on a fire.

A pot of coffee cooked in the flames.

"We can make Riverton by six o'clock or so tonight," Lang said as he dismounted.

Rosa filled a cup with coffee and handed it to Lang.

"I crossed the westbound tracks about an hour north of here," Lang said. "The railroad depot probably sits just outside of town, but I doubt it will be open after six. Most trains out here run a morning and afternoon schedule."

"We would have to spend the night in town," Rosa said.

"Too risky," Lang said. "We'll camp about an hour south of town, and I'll ride into the station at first light. They usually have a schedule posted on a board outside the office. Hopefully there will be a train west tomorrow sometime."

"It has been a long few weeks," Rosa said.

"Yes, it has," Lang said. "If there's a train tomorrow, you and the boy put on the best clothes Mr. Daves provided and dump the rest. Before the train leaves, pick up some new clothes at the dry mills store in town. That scissors you have, cut his hair short so he blends in more on the train."

Rosa turned away, knelt before the fire, and turned the hens on the spit. "I suppose there is no point to asking you to change your mind?" she said.

"No, but if I pick up paper and pencil at the station, you could do me the favor of writing a statement to the court," Lang said.

Rosa stirred the fire. "You are such a fool," she said softly.

Cox was stunned to find Grey Wolf's horse dead on the trail. The Apache warrior's reputation in that he could ride very long distances without food, water, or rest was totally warranted.

Grey Wolf rode most of the night and opened up a thirty-six-hour lead on him, until this point in a valley of grazing pasture. Somehow, his horse caught his right hoof in a gopher hole, fell hard, and broke the leg.

Grey Wolf didn't waste a bullet but killed his horse with the blade of his knife, slicing open the animal's neck.

The horse had been dead at least twenty-four hours, and the vultures and wolves were having a field day with the carcass.

Grey Wolf took his supplies and Winchester rifle, but left the saddle. He walked north along a road.

Cox followed the trail.

In a box canyon, someone in a wagon stopped to fix a broken wheel. It appeared Lang, the woman, and boy had stumbled upon the wagon, helped repair the wheel, and rode off to the west.

Grey Wolf followed on foot.

And returned on foot and followed the road.

Cox mounted his horse and led Lang's horse and the mule along the road, following Grey Wolf's tracks.

The trail of wagon tracks and Grey Wolf's footprints went on for half the day into the late afternoon until the wagon turned off onto a narrow dirt road.

Grey Wolf followed.

A mile or so down the dirt road, a ranch came into view.

Grey Wolf walked onto the ranch.

At the entrance of the ranch there was an archway with a hanging sign made of wood.

Daves Ranch was burned into the sign.

Cox dismounted and tied Lang's horse and the mule to the fence post beside the archway. Then he mounted his horse and rode the half mile to the ranch house.

He dismounted again and tied his horse to a post at the corral. The corral was empty of horses.

Cox removed the Winchester rifle from the saddle, cocked the lever, and walked to the porch steps.

"Hello inside?" he said loudly.

Cox half expected to see an old-timer with a shotgun come busting through the door, but his greeting was met with silence.

He took the steps to the porch and cautiously pushed against the door with the Winchester. The door was unlocked and he pushed it inward.

Standing in the threshold, Cox shouted, "Anybody home? My name is Marshal John Cox. Mr. Daves?"

Cox stepped into the cabin and stood in the living room. A stone fireplace was the focal point in the room. A table with chairs, a rocking chair, a bookcase filled with books, and a small desk were the main furnishings.

To the right was a pantry. Cox entered the pantry where

shelves were stacked with canned goods, flour, and coffee. He inspected the goods and determined that several cans were missing.

There was a door in the pantry that led to the side of the cabin, but it was locked from the inside.

Cox left the pantry and went to the hallway off the living room that led to the bedrooms.

In the archway of the main bedroom, an old man lay dead on the floor. He cradled a shotgun, but he never got the chance to use it. His skull was split open by Grey Wolf's tomahawk. His scalp had been taken by Grey Wolf's knife.

Cox checked the other two bedrooms. He found three dead men, boys, really, between the ages of sixteen and twenty. They, like their father, were killed by the tomahawk and scalped by the knife.

He sighed heavily, feeling the weight of the world pressing hard on his soul.

"You murdering savage," Cox said aloud.

He went outside to breathe some fresh air to clear his head. There were about four hours of daylight left. He used the time to dig graves behind the house where a family cemetery was located.

From their campsite, they could see the lights of Riverton twinkle in the distance. They were an hour's ride south of the town.

They camped an hour before dark, and Lang and Joaquin went off to hunt a chicken or a hare for supper.

Rosa had clean paper and a new pencil in her satchel, and she used the time alone to compose a letter to the courts on Lang's behalf.

By the time Lang and Joaquin returned with two chickens and some eggs for the morning, she had penned a three-page letter addressed to the courts.

She didn't mention the letter until after they had eaten and Joaquin was asleep beside the fire. Then she removed the folded pages from her satchel and handed them to Lang.

"I had paper and pencil," she said. "In case there is no time in the morning."

Lang took the papers and looked at Rosa.

"If it is not satisfactory, I will make changes," Rosa said. "In the morning. I am tired and am going to sleep."

Cox found a large cot in the storage shed behind the house and assembled it in the living room beside the fireplace.

He made a fire in the kitchen cooking stove and found fresh meats in the icebox where a slab of ice on the bottom kept foods fresh.

He cooked a steak with beans and made coffee. He ate in silence at the table. Then he took coffee in a chair before the fireplace and listened to the crackle of the fire.

Cox removed his pipe and tobacco pouch, but when he went to fill the bowl, his hands started to shake and he burst into sudden tears.

Lang read Rosa's letter. In it she exonerated him of the murders at the stagecoach relay station. She named George and his two friends as the killers. She stated they took her and her son, violated her, and tied the two of them up before riding off with the money they stole from Alfred Wallace.

She explained how Lang had saved her from the coach and helped her and her son escape from Grey Wolf.

She ended by requesting from the courts the opportunity to speak at Lang's trial.

Lang folded the papers and placed them into his saddlebags.

He rolled a cigarette and smoked, looking at the slightly larger moon in the sky.

"Well, you certainly are a fool," he said aloud softly.

Chapter Forty-Three

Lang and Joaquin stood with the two horses a hundred feet behind the railroad station and watched Rosa as she walked away from them.

She wore one of the dresses provided by Daves and had pinned her long hair up in a fashionable bun.

Lang thought how handsome a woman she was as she walked to the station and disappeared from view.

She wasn't gone long enough to buy the tickets.

Her face appeared distraught.

"What?" Lang asked when Rosa returned.

"Grey Wolf," she said.

"He's here?" Lang asked.

"No. He's burning the railroad tracks," Rosa said. "The man in the office said it would take weeks to repair the tracks he's burned all across Colorado and Wyoming, into New Mexico Territory and even Nebraska."

"Wait here," Lang said.

He walked to the station. On the schedule board where times and destinations should have been listed was a public notice. The notice read that service had been interrupted until further notice due to tracks being set on fire by the renegade Grey Wolf and his followers.

"Son of a bitch," Lang said aloud.

He didn't bother entering the office but returned to Rosa and the boy.

"What do we do now?" Rosa asked.

"Still got fresh paper?" Lang said.

Rosa nodded.

"Give me a sheet and the pencil. I'll make a list of supplies we'll need."

Rosa came out of the general store carrying two large sacks of supplies. She carried the heavy sacks to where Lang and Joaquin were hiding in a field outside of town. They were seated against a tree in the shade while the horses grazed.

They stood and Lang took the sacks.

"What I can't fit in the saddlebags, put in your satchel," Lang said.

"And where are we going with all these supplies?" Rosa asked.

Lang pulled out the map and opened it against the saddle of his horse. He traced a path with his finger.

"Through the Big Horn Mountains, through the Hole in the Wall pass, and then east to the town of Cody," Lang said. "A few miles north of Cody is an army outpost. I can turn you and the boy over to the army and . . ."

"But what about California?" Rosa asked.

"I know what we planned, but we didn't count on Grey Wolf and his band burning railroad tracks all across the territory," Lang said.

"But the army . . ."

"Can protect you," Lang said. "I can't. Not against Grey Wolf's entire bunch. Neither can this town, even if they were so inclined. Once Grey Wolf is apprehended or killed, you and the boy can go to California in peace."

"And you?"

"Now is not the time to worry about me."

Rosa stared at Lang.

"How long to Cody?" she finally asked.

"Eight days if we make good time through the pass," Lang said. "Six days to reach the Hole in the Wall. Best change out of that dress and put on your riding pants."

Cox ate a full breakfast and then loaded up on extra supplies from the pantry before he left the Daves ranch.

At the corral, he saddled his horse and Lang's and then loaded the supplies onto the mule.

Before riding out, he inspected the tracks. Grey Wolf had emptied the corral of horses, scattering them to the fields. He'd probably selected the largest horse for himself, saddled him from the cluster of saddles hung across the railings, and headed back to the road.

And Cox followed.

"Is there fresh water between here and the pass?" Rosa asked when they stopped to noon.

"A lot of streams running off the mountains this time of year," Lang said. "Water will be no problem."

Rosa nodded. "I'll make a fire."

While Rosa and Joaquin made a fire and broke out the cookware, Lang sifted through the supplies. They had beans, bacon, fresh biscuits, and canned fruit. Lang and Rosa drank coffee. Joaquin enjoyed one of several bottles of soda pop, something called sarsaparilla.

Afterward, Lang smoked a cigarette and finished a cup of coffee. Rosa sat next to him and looked at the mountains in the distance.

"Grey Wolf is not with his men burning the tracks," she said softly. "He has used this trick before when planning a raid. He has cut off our escape by the railroad, but he is not with his men. He is following us. I can feel him and he is not far behind."

Lang looked at Rosa.

"He will catch us," she said. "And there is nothing we can do about it."

Lang suddenly stood up. "Yes, there is," he said. "We can ride."

Cox inspected Grey Wolf's tracks on the road. The Apache had a full two-day lead on him, but on an uncertain horse. A horse that might not be up to the task of the brutal pace Grey Wolf was going to put him through.

Cox rode all day, stopping briefly to rest the horses and mule, to feed and water them, taking just some biscuits for himself.

He rode until close to sunset.

He tended to the horses and mule and then built a fire to cook some supper.

He ate with the crackling of the fire for company.

Afterward, Cox spread out his bedroll and watched the waxing moon and clusters of stars, and that's when it struck him funny.

He was no longer pursuing Emmet Lang the outlaw, but Grey Wolf the Apache.

Chapter Forty-Four

The two cowboys herding several hundred head of cattle to fresh grazing land stopped to fix a hot lunch after seven straight hours in the saddle.

It was to be their downfall.

While they ate a hot meal and drank coffee, they were totally unaware that Grey Wolf was observing them from a thicket of tall grass less than one hundred feet behind them.

They carried Colt revolvers, but neither of the cowboys were gunmen. The most they ever shot at were rattlers and such. As they lazed in the sun with second cups of coffee, their horses grazing in the field about fifty feet from them suddenly whinnied nervously.

The cowboys looked at their horses.

The horses neighed and shook their heads.

"Could be a rattler nearby," one of the cowboys said.

"Let's take a look," the other cowboy said.

They stood up and heard a noise behind them. They turned and faced the sun, which was now in the west.

They squinted at the figure of a man that was blurred in the sun.

"This is private land," one of the cowboys said. "Those are Bar T cattle."

Grey Wolf moved forward and the cowboys could see him clearly now. He was bare-chested and the largest man they had ever seen. A tomahawk was held loosely in his right hand.

He appeared to be an Apache.

"What the hell . . . ?" a cowboy said.

Grey Wolf broke into a run and brought the tomahawk up over his head.

For a brief moment, the cowboys were stunned.

In that brief moment, Grey Wolf covered fifty feet of ground.

Shocked into action, the cowboys clumsily grabbed for their Colt revolvers.

Grey Wolf roared his Apache war cry and reached the cowboys as they fumbled with their guns. Grey Wolf leapt high into the air and struck one cowboy on the top of his skull with the tomahawk.

As the cowboy fell dead, Grey Wolf spun in a circle and slammed the second cowboy in the chest with the blade of the tomahawk.

The cowboy gasped. As blood ran down his chest, he looked at Grey Wolf.

Calmly, Grey Wolf yanked the tomahawk from the cowboy's chest, then screamed his war cry again and split the cowboy's skull wide open with the tomahawk.

Chapter Forty-Five

"You mind telling me just what in the hell we're doing up like we was a pair of nesting jayhawks?" Curly Johnson asked.

Johnson and Hatfield were prone on a cliff a thousand feet high about two miles from the hideaway cabins.

"Keeping watch like George said," Hatfield said. "For once, I agree with him. We got to watch the pass until the snow flies and boards it up for the winter."

"And while we're here with our peckers in the dirt, what's George doing but riding over to Cody to wiggle his bean," Johnson said.

"We needed extra supplies, and he said he was going to see about a whore," Hatfield said. "Besides, I feel safer with him gone than here. Now do something useful and make us some coffee."

Johnson stood up and walked to their horses. He removed the coffee pot, water, and a bag of coffee from the saddlebags.

He built a fire and set the coffee to boil, then returned to Hatfield.

"Ain't nobody going to come," Johnson said. "There's a night frost this high up and less than a month until the snows will come and lock anybody looking to come in on the outside."

"True, but in the meantime, it's a good idea to keep watch and see who we might be sharing the winter with," Hatfield said. "How's that coffee coming?"

Johnson went to the boiling pot of coffee, filled two tin cups, and carried them back to Hatfield.

"Tell you what I think," Johnson said as he gave Hatfield a cup. "I think the only one George is afraid of seeing enter the pass is Emmet Lang. That's what I think."

Cox was correct when he thought the horse Grey Wolf took from the Daves ranch wasn't up to the mark. The Apache rode the horse nearly to ground until the exhausted horse could go no more.

Then Grey Wolf abandoned the animal and set out on foot with the saddle.

Cox tracked Grey Wolf's footprints for about five miles to a range where three hundred or so head of cattle peacefully grazed.

In the mix of cattle were two horses.

Cox dismounted and allowed his horse, along with Lang's horse and the mule, to graze. He cautiously approached the two stray horses. The cattle paid him little mind, but the two horses whinnied a bit at his approach.

One horse was saddled, the other was not.

Cox slowly pulled his Colt revolver and cocked the hammer. He scanned the area and spotted the buzzards on the other side of the grazing cattle.

He didn't need to walk to the buzzards to know what he would find.

"It's close to dark, Smiley," Johnson said. "Let's head back. Ain't no one coming. Besides, I want to talk something over with you."

"Pack up our gear, and we'll talk on the way," Hatfield said.

A few minutes later, they rode along the ridge back to the cabins.

"What's on your mind, Curly?" Hatfield asked.

"I can't shake that feeling George is going to kill us and keep all the money for himself," Johnson said.

"I know," Hatfield said. "I'm feeling that way myself."

"Well, we can't set us up as a pair of sitting ducks for George to pick off," Johnson said. "What do we do?"

"George should be back late afternoon tomorrow," Hatfield said. "Let's watch the pass to Cody and see if he returns with a wagonload of supplies like he said. If we still don't trust him, we can kill him before he kills us and ride the hell out of here in one piece."

"After we divide up George's share of the money?" Johnson said.

"Of course."

Cox buried the two cowboys in separate graves. He marked each grave with a cross made of wood sticks. When they were both in the ground, he said a prayer and then made camp for the night.

While supper cooked, he tended the horses. The horse that belonged to one of the cowboys was a large male with a powerful chest and thick, sturdy legs. For Grey Wolf to have chosen the other cowboy's horse meant it was a superior animal, one he could ride hard without worry.

Grey Wolf had lost time, and he wanted to make up the ground. He would ride nonstop to catch Lang, who, Cox estimated with the lost time, was five or six days ahead of him.

After eating, Cox dug out his writing paper and pencil and wrote a note and placed it under a rock beside the graves.

It was the best he could do for now until he reached a town with a telegraph office.

The half moon slowly rose above the mountains and Cox watched it for a while as he smoked his pipe.

From what he knew of Grey Wolf, the Apache liked to

conduct his raids on a full moon night.

It would be a full moon in less than a week.

Chapter Forty-Six

"We need to camp early," Lang said as he dismounted beside a stream running down from the mountains. "Our horses need rest and grain."

"My back is killing me," Rosa said as she and Joaquin dismounted.

"We've made good time," Lang said. "Three days, and we'll be inside the pass."

Rosa walked to the stream. She picked up a pebble and tossed it into the water. "It's deep enough for me to take a bath while the sun is still on it," she said.

"You go ahead while I build a fire," Lang said.

Rosa removed a bar of soap and a small glass bottle of shampoo that she'd purchased at the Riverton general store. At the water's edge, she stripped and walked into the water and then dove under.

Then she swam to the shore for the bar of soap and spoke to Joaquin in Apache.

The boy started to remove his clothes.

Lang looked at Joaquin. "You see a stream and automatically it's Saturday night bath time, huh?" he said.

Joaquin looked at Lang, then finished removing his clothes and dove into the water.

"A bath wouldn't hurt you none, Mr. Lang," Rosa said.

Lang turned to look at her. She was neck deep, lathering her hair with the shampoo.

"What's that in your hair?" he asked.

"Soap made just for hair," Rosa said. "It's called shampoo. I saw it in the general store. You should try it."

"Let me get the fire going first," Lang said.

After building a good-sized campfire, Lang put a pot of coffee on to percolate. He looked at Rosa and Joaquin. She was wading around, and the boy was scrubbing his hair with the hair soap.

"Coming?" Rosa teased.

"As soon as you turn around," Lang said.

Rosa swam away and gave Lang her back. He stripped quickly and slowly waded into the cold stream waters.

"Water's so cold it hurts," Lang said.

"Don't be such a little girl, Mr. Lang," Rosa said. "A little cold water never hurt anybody. Catch."

Rosa tossed Lang the bar of soap.

"Don't forget to wash behind your ears," she said.

Riding south through the Big Horn Mountains, George didn't bother to hurry the horse pulling the wagon loaded with extra supplies. He wasn't followed out of Cody, and as far as he knew, the secret pass through the notch in the mountains was still known only to a select few outlaws.

Riding into Cody, George fully intended to kill Johnson and Hatfield upon his return to the pass. They were stupid, greedy men with no notion of how to spend their money or live lives as rich men.

They'd served their purpose, and now it was time for them to go. He figured to stay the winter on his own and ride north in the spring.

In Cody, he had a shave and a bath and read the *Cheyenne Ledger* while he soaked in the tub. The news was grave. According to one story, Grey Wolf and his men were burning railroad tracks all across the territory, supposedly to prevent his wife from escaping by train. US Marshals, sheriffs, and the army all were conducting searches for the wife and son of Grey Wolf and the outlaw Emmet Lang.

The newspaper was just three days old.

Lang was still at large and running not just from the law, but from Grey Wolf.

George was counting on the law, or that savage, to dispense with Lang, but by the news accounts, Emmet was still at large.

He was smart, Emmet was, and in his place, George knew exactly what he would do to escape the law and that savage Grey Wolf.

He would go to the Hole in the Wall and sit out the winter.

So now, George needed Johnson and Hatfield if, as George suspected, Lang was on his way to the pass.

Johnson and Hatfield weren't much as gunmen went, but they could act as lookouts in the pass and anybody, including those two idiots, could get off a lucky shot.

He had no choice but to keep them around for a while.

At least until Emmet Lang was dead and in the ground.

Lang watched the moon rise slowly in the sky. It was close to three quarters full and would be nearly a perfect circle by the time they were inside the pass. Grey Wolf or the law hadn't caught up to them, and he was starting to believe they could make it to Cody in one piece.

The night air was chilled and without a fire; Lang was glad for the blankets Mr. Daves had provided.

He looked at Rosa and Joaquin a few feet away from him. They were huddled together for warmth under two blankets, sleeping soundly.

With his saddle for a pillow, Lang rolled a cigarette and smoked, watching the stars. Coming into the fall sky, they were bright and too numerous to count. As a young boy, he would often sit on the porch of the farmhouse and watch the stars. His father knew all the constellations and planets and taught him their names and movements.

What fascinated his father most was the moon. He would often set up the old spyglass on a tripod and study its surface at night. Lang would sometimes join him for his nighttime hobby, and they would look at the craters and rocky surface of the moon.

His father taught him a simple trick to tell if a partial moon was waxing or waning at a glance. If the right side of the moon was lit, it was waxing. The left side, it was waning.

Lang put out the spent cigarette and closed his eyes. He was exhausted, but his mind was still racing with thoughts, and sleep wouldn't come.

The moon crawled along the sky. He estimated the time at around ten in the evening. As a child, on nights he had difficulty sleeping, his mother would warm a glass of milk, and it would lull him to sleep.

Lang didn't have a warm glass of milk, so he rolled another cigarette.

And listened to the soft breeze blowing down from the mountains.

Rosa or Joaquin turned in their sleep.

Lang inhaled on the cigarette and blew a ring that rose up and drifted away on the soft breeze.

Leaves rustled, and the sound of a twig snapping caused him to turn to his left. In the pale moonlight, he saw Rosa walking away from camp with a blanket wrapped around her shoulders.

Lang sat up.

Rosa paused and looked back at him, then turned and vanished.

Lang stood up and walked to the point where Rosa disappeared, turned to his left, and followed her.

He walked about fifty feet and stopped when he saw her standing in the moonlight beside a tall tree.

She was watching him, waiting for him.

As Lang approached her, Rosa let the blanket fall away from her shoulders.

He stopped a few feet from her and they made eye contact.

Then Lang took her in his arms and they came together in an anxious, passionate kiss that left them breathless.

When they finally came apart, Rosa reached for the top button of her blouse. She looked at Lang and said, "What took you so long?"

Chapter Forty-Seven

"We figured you wouldn't be back until the morning," Johnson said.

"No reason to wait, boys," George said. "Not even a decent whore in the whole town of Cody."

They were at the table in their cabin with plates of stew and cups of whiskey.

"And I brought back something a mite better than this swill you call whiskey," George said.

He reached down beside his leg and picked up a bottle of Tennessee sipping whiskey. "Five dollars a bottle," he said. "I got six of them at the saloon they call an emporium."

"Six ain't going to last till spring, George," Johnson said.

"We got plenty of this crap we've been drinking if it runs out," George said. "How was the pass? See anybody?"

"Not even a stray dog," Hatfield said. "We figure no one is going to risk getting snowed in so close to winter."

"Even so, we need to keep watch every day until the snow flies," George said. "If we're going to have neighbors all winter, we best know who they are ahead of time. Any more of this stew?"

"Pot's still half full," Johnson said.

"Why don't you dish us out another plate while I open this fine bottle of sipping whiskey," George said.

★ ★ ★ ★ ★

Lang opened his eyes to the aroma of coffee and bacon sizzling in a pan. Rosa was stirring the bacon with a fork and looked at him when he stood up.

"The coffee is hot," Rosa said. "Joaquin went to find some eggs."

Lang filled a tin mug with coffee and took a small sip. "About last night," he said.

"I'm not sorry it happened," Rosa said. "Are you?"

"No."

"Then there is nothing to discuss. Here comes Joaquin with the eggs."

Cox studied Grey Wolf's tracks. The horse he stole from the cowboy was large and powerful, with a left-leaning gait even when running in a straight line.

Grey Wolf had made up most of the time he'd lost by riding hard through the night, judging from the tracks in the grass. Lang appeared headed to Riverton, so that's where Grey Wolf would go, and Cox would follow.

Riverton was a railroad town. Maybe Lang was planning to put the woman and boy on a train, maybe go with them.

Even Grey Wolf couldn't track a train.

Grey Wolf had probably figured that out, and that was the reason for his hard riding.

Cox mounted his horse, and with Lang's horse and the mule in tow, followed Grey Wolf's tracks.

"How far to this pass?" Rosa asked when they took a short break to rest the horses and eat a cold lunch of biscuits and jerky.

"Two, maybe two and a half days' ride to reach the pass," Lang said. "Another two to reach the hideout. We can rest there for a few days before riding to Cody."

"And while I give myself and Joaquin to the army, you do what?" Rosa asked.

"Cody doesn't have a marshal, but they've got a sheriff," Lang said. "I'll give myself up to him, and he can send to Cheyenne for a marshal. I figure, like I said, to get maybe three years. Maybe less if a judge considers your letter."

"So last night meant nothing to you," Rosa said.

"I didn't say that," Lang said. "But what choice do I have? Sooner or later, the law will catch up to me. It's better sooner than later. My first priority right now is to get you and the boy to safety."

"You didn't answer my question," Rosa said.

"By God but you're a stubborn woman," Lang said.

"Let's ride," Rosa said. "You can think about the right answer on the way."

Grey Wolf sat beside his horse, ate a cold supper, and looked at the lights of Riverton less than a mile away.

The tracks of Lang and the horse ridden by his wife and son led directly to the town. They didn't take the road, but came up from the west so they wouldn't be seen and probably went directly to the railroad.

From there he would pick up their tracks come morning. In four nights would come the full moon, the silver moon. It would be full for three nights before it began to wane.

Then he would kill this outlaw Lang and his wife, and his son would sit by his side and grow to a man.

And Grey Wolf's heart would be full again.

After making love for the second time in two nights, Rosa rolled off Lang and nestled her head against his chest.

"I need to ask you something," she said when she caught her breath.

"Ask," Lang said.

"Do you care for me?" Rosa asked.

"Both you and the boy," Lang said.

"That's not what I meant," Rosa said.

"I know," Lang said. "In our present situation, it would be foolish of both of us to pretend we're going anywhere else but where we're going. You and the boy to the army. Me off to prison. Let's just leave it at that."

Rosa turned her head so that Lang wouldn't see the tears forming in her eyes.

"We better get back before Joaquin wakes up and finds us gone," she said.

Chapter Forty-Eight

Grey Wolf waited behind the outhouse for the man who sold tickets inside the railroad station to come out.

Why did the white man always take so long to do his business? Grey Wolf wondered.

Finally he heard the man pulling up his pants. Grey Wolf removed his long knife from its sheath and held it in his left hand. In the right hand, he held his tomahawk.

The door of the outhouse opened and Grey Wolf surprised the man by placing the blade of his knife just inches from his throat.

"Make a sound and I will slit you like a hog," Grey Wolf said.

The man, frightened out of his wits, looked at Grey Wolf.

"Did a Mexican woman try to buy a ticket at your station?" Grey Wolf asked. "Dark hair and eyes, maybe with a boy?"

The man nodded.

"When?"

"Five days ago, but she was alone."

"Are you sure?"

"She was alone when she came into the office. I can't speak for after that. I did see her enter the general store, but I didn't see her leave town."

"Are you sure?" Grey Wolf asked.

The man nodded.

"Thank you," Grey Wolf said and slit the man's throat.

★ ★ ★ ★ ★

Cox rode into Riverton in the late afternoon and was immediately aware that every citizen on the street was watching him. He knew he must have looked a sight, but not much different than the average cowboy after weeks on the trail.

He rode to the sheriff's office and tied his horse, Lang's horse, and the mule to a hitching post.

Cox stretched his aching, sore back and then took the steps to the wood plank sidewalk and opened the door to the sheriff's office.

A man too young to be an elected sheriff sat behind the desk.

"I'm United States Marshal John Cox. Who is sheriff of this town?" Cox asked.

"That would be Sheriff Dan Winstone," the man said. "I'm Deputy Evans."

"Well, Deputy Evans, where is Sheriff Winstone?" Cox asked.

"At the undertaker," Evans said. "We had us a murder this morning."

"In the outhouse?" Cox said, somewhat surprised.

"Just outside, and then it looks like he was lowered to the seat," Sheriff Winstone said. "Judging by the amount of blood in the dirt outside the door."

Cox and Winstone were walking from the undertaker's office to the outhouse behind the train depot.

"Any strangers in town this morning not here this afternoon?" Cox asked as they approached the outhouse.

"Probably a dozen or more," Winstone said. "Usually it's more, but with the railroad out of commission, we—"

"Out of commission why?" Cox asked.

"How long have you been in the bush, Marshal?" Winstone asked.

"Weeks."

"That explains it," Winstone said. "Marshal, Grey Wolf and his band have been burning railroad tracks all across the west for ten days or more now. Service is down in six states on most lines, including here."

Cox paused for a second as his mind raced.

"Grey Wolf's men may be out there burning tracks, but Grey Wolf isn't with them," Cox said.

"How do you know that?" Winstone asked.

"Because I've been tracking him since the Overland way station south of Denver, and his tracks lead right to your doorstep," Cox said. "Or should I say outhouse."

They reached the outhouse.

"Grey Wolf, here? Why?" Winstone asked.

"He's tracking his wife and an outlaw named Emmet Lang," Cox said. "And I'm tracking them."

Winstone stared at Cox.

"Is there a place I can get a decent steak and a room for the night?" Cox asked. "My back needs a night off from sleeping on the ground."

"The railroad owns the best hotel in town," Winstone said. "It's near empty right now."

Cox nodded. "Good."

After a shave, a hot bath, and a change of clothes, Cox met Winstone in the hotel dining room. Both ordered a steak.

"I read the newspapers while I took a bath," Cox said. "A lot's happened."

"Want me to form a posse?" Winstone asked. "Grey Wolf can't be more than twelve hours ahead of us by now."

"He can ride two miles to your one, and he never stops," Cox said. "No, no posse. I'll continue alone in the morning."

"Alone? After that savage? We could send a wire to—"

"It wouldn't do any good," Cox said. "This is a job for an

entire army or one man. I started it alone, and I'll finish it alone."

Winstone nodded. "I hope you know what you're doing."

"Me, too," Cox said. "What do they have for pie in this hotel?"

After breakfast with Winstone and restocking his supplies, Cox tracked Grey Wolf's tracks west out of Riverton.

Grey Wolf was headed for the Big Horn Mountains.

Chapter Forty-Nine

"Another half day and we're in the pass," Lang said. "There might be a lookout during the day, but not at night. We'll be able to make a fire tonight. Two days' ride from the entrance is the hideout. We can rest a day in a cabin. Two days from there is Cody."

They were resting the horses in the shade of a large tree.

Rosa sipped water from a cup. "What if the hideout is occupied?" she asked.

"I'll see it, and we'll ride straight through to Cody," Lang said.

"If we can see the lookout, so will Grey Wolf," Rosa said.

"If there is one, we won't see them until we're a few miles from the cabin," Lang said. "When we reach that point, we'll travel at night by the moon. He'll figure that out and do the same. We'll know the cabins are occupied by the horses in the corral and lights in the cabin."

Rosa looked at Joaquin, who was brushing the horses.

"If Grey Wolf catches us before we reach Cody, I want you to do something for me," she said.

"What?"

"He can't take us alive," Rosa said. "Me and Joaquin."

Lang stared at her.

"Promise me that much," Rosa said.

"I can't promise that," Lang said.

"You don't know what Grey Wolf is capable of," Rosa said.

"If you feel anything for me and Joaquin at all, you will promise me."

Lang looked away. "I promise," he said.

As the day wore on, the pass narrowed. Eventually, where it turned off to the cabins, the pass was wide enough just for one to ride at a time.

At dark, they stopped and made camp for the night.

"We're in the pass," Lang said. "Tomorrow afternoon we can start to worry."

Grey Wolf wasn't at all worried about covering his tracks or trying to throw Cox off his trail. The Apache simply rode.

Cox inspected the tracks left by Grey Wolf. They were twenty-four-hours old. He was riding directly into the Big Horn Mountains.

That meant Lang, the woman, and the boy were riding into the Big Horn Mountains.

Whatever for?

Those mountains were hard, unforgiving country. No place for a woman and a boy, or a US Marshal for that matter.

Lang had a plan.

He wasn't just riding to escape the law and Grey Wolf, but he had a specific reason for where he was headed.

There was only one way to find out what that was: to keep on his trail.

Rosa waited for Joaquin to fall asleep before she sneaked away from their camp with a blanket wrapped around her shoulders.

Under a bright, three-quarter moon, Lang followed her about a hundred feet and found her seated on the blanket.

"I don't know what I want more, your touch or your promise," Rosa said.

"You have them both," Lang said as he sat beside her.

"If the army will allow it, I will testify on your behalf before the court, and then I will take Joaquin west to California because I don't think they or the law will capture Grey Wolf," Rosa said. "He will take revenge against my family in Mexico for betraying him, and the army or the Mexican law will not stop him. He will take his men across the border and kill them all. I will have to live with the sin that I chose the life of my son over the lives of my family."

Lang sighed heavily. He pulled out his tobacco pouch and paper and rolled a cigarette. "Mexico might be behind the times, but they do have telegraph stations and an army. The commander of the outpost can wire the Mexican officials and have your family protected."

"The way they prevented him from burning the railroad tracks," Rosa said. "The army and every lawman in the west are looking for Grey Wolf, and yet he is probably no more than three or four days behind us."

"We'll ride straight through the pass to Cody," Lang said. "The terms of my surrender will be, besides myself, to give up the names of George and the others in exchange for arranging to have your family protected and moved to safety. And a report on the illegal activities of Alfred Wallace of the Indian Affairs Agency, something they'll be very interested in."

"The army will do that?" Rosa asked.

"When an army officer gives his word, it is never broken," Lang said. "I know a little about that."

"That's right, you do," Rosa said. "Captain."

Lang struck a match and lit the cigarette.

"You would sacrifice yourself for me and Joaquin," Rosa said. "Because?"

"I'm tired of running," Lang said. "I'm tired of being a lazy man. I'm willing to pay the price for a fresh start."

Rosa looked at Lang. "Because?"

"You don't leave a man much room," Lang said.

"I've been an Apache slave for half my life," Rosa said. "I don't have a lot of room to give."

"The words won't change our situation," Lang said.

"Because?" Rosa said.

"By God, you're a stubborn woman."

"Because?" Rosa said.

Lang stared at her.

"God won't strike you dead if you say the words," Rosa said.

Lang sighed. "Yes, I do love you," he said.

Rosa looked up at the sky, then lowered her eyes and smiled. "See? No lightning bolt," she said.

"I don't know what it amounts to," Lang said.

"If we live through this, I will wait for you no matter how long it takes," Rosa said. "That's what it amounts to."

"More than I deserve," Lang said.

Rosa sat on the blanket.

"Do you plan to stand there and talk all night?" she asked.

Chapter Fifty

Night watch made no sense, Johnson thought as he stood on a cliff a few miles south of the cabins.

George said that Lang was smart enough to know to travel at night when the moon was nearly full and the pass was illuminated enough to traverse.

George actually used that word, traverse.

Johnson didn't know what the word meant and asked Hatfield.

Hatfield thought it meant ride.

In any case, George worked out a schedule so the pass would be covered every hour of the day and night.

George had first watch from dawn to midday. Hatfield took over until midnight. Johnson got stuck with the third watch.

He made a fire far enough away from the cliff so that it couldn't be seen below and put on a pot of coffee to boil.

When the coffee was ready, he took a cup to the cliff and smoked a cigarette.

Looking down, Johnson could see the floor of the pass clearly enough so that if a rider came through, he would see him.

Maybe George was right about that, except that Johnson didn't believe anybody would be foolish enough to lose sleep and travel at night.

Grey Wolf made up lost time by riding day and night until the cowboy's horse simply dropped dead on him.

The end for the horse came quickly. It slowed, wobbled, snorted, and then fell over dead. At the last second, Grey Wolf jumped off before the horse hit the ground.

He removed the saddle and then made a fire. With his knife, he sliced meat off the horse and cooked it on sticks.

As he ate, Grey Wolf decided his best option was to wait. The lawman couldn't be more than a day and a half behind him, and if he was to catch the outlaw and his traitorous wife, he needed a horse.

He still had some whiskey left, and he sipped from the bottle while he smoked his pipe in front of the fire.

The white man's horses were weak. That was just one more reason to hate them.

Grey Wolf looked at the moon. It was three quarters full. He wanted to end this chase before the waning cycle began in six nights, so he couldn't afford to lose more than one day without a horse.

He sipped whiskey and watched the moon.

Seated in front of the campfire, Cox composed two letters, one to each of his daughters. He told each of them that he would like to come for a visit soon, and that he planned to retire at age fifty.

Cox didn't know when he would mail the letters, probably not until he came to another town. That could be weeks.

He folded each letter carefully and tucked them into the thin box of writing paper. He didn't have envelopes. That would have to wait until he reached a town.

Cox placed the box of paper in his saddlebags and then stuffed his pipe and lit it with a twig from the fire.

A thought occurred to him, and Cox brought out the box of writing paper again. He selected a clean sheet and pencil.

He stared at the paper for many long minutes.

Then he moistened the tip of the pencil with his tongue and wrote, *Last Will and Testament.*

Chapter Fifty-One

Grey Wolf ate a breakfast of roasted horse meat and water. Before sunrise, he was on the move and walked south, backtracking.

He carried his Winchester rifle, tomahawk and knife, and canteen, leaving his saddle and bags behind.

He walked without stopping to rest until the sun was in the noon position. Then Grey Wolf rested for a few minutes and drank some water. He continued walking and didn't stop again until close to sundown.

He drank water and rested until the sun had set.

After checking his position, Grey Wolf started walking again and didn't stop until he spotted the red dot of a campfire.

He sat and watched the red dot until it started to fade. Then he stood and moved slowly and silently toward the dwindling campfire.

The lawman was asleep inside a bedroll with a rifle cradled in his arms. The fire was nearly out, but the moon was bright enough to see his face. The man was older than Grey Wolf expected, but that he'd kept pace with Grey Wolf and outsmarted him that night with the fire meant he was hearty and dangerous.

The horses were closer than the lawman. Grey Wolf moved silently to the horses and mule and inspected the horses. Both were hobbled, but bridled. He selected the larger of the two, a massive black horse.

With his knife, Grey Wolf sliced away the leather strips that hobbled his legs, took the reins, and quietly walked the horse away from the lawman's camp. He thought about going back and killing the lawman.

He decided not to waste time. He could always kill the lawman later after the outlaw and his wife were dead, if the lawman was still around.

He walked a few hundred feet, then mounted the horse bareback and rode north.

For the second night in a row, Johnson drew the midnight shift watching the cliffs. It was easy enough duty if you didn't mind the chilly night air, lack of conversation, and loss of sleep.

Hatfield had made a fire. Johnson kept it going and made a fresh pot of coffee. He had supper at the cabin, but he brought a sack of biscuits and some jerked beef to last until breakfast.

He sipped coffee and munched on a hard biscuit as he stood watch over the pass.

After eating the biscuit, Johnson rolled a cigarette and sat near the fire to keep warm.

"Ain't nobody gonna come," he said aloud.

The horse was every bit the equal of his horse he'd had to put down, Grey Wolf thought as the powerful animal opened his stride on command.

Grey Wolf rode hard and the horse didn't tire. Within a few hours, they arrived at the campsite where he had abandoned his saddle.

He allowed the horse to rest and cool down.

Grey Wolf took some water and then smoked his pipe. It struck him odd that the lawman was traveling with two horses. The white man often traveled with a mule to carry supplies, as they were too inept and weak to live off the land, but why bring a riderless horse that would only slow you down?

The lawman had a purpose and a plan, but Grey Wolf couldn't waste time worrying about it now.

Maybe he would ask the lawman this question right before he killed him.

Chapter Fifty-Two

Lang rested the horses around two in the morning. He opened two cans of peaches from the bag of supplies, and they ate the snack with sips of water.

"A few miles ahead, the pass narrows and winds," Lang said. "A few miles past that are the cabins of the hideaway. We'll ride without stopping until morning and find a place to camp and get some sleep. If we make it past the cabins without seeing a lookout, chances are we won't see one until we're out of the Big Horns."

"What if we see a lookout?" Rosa asked. "Won't he see us?"

"We'll walk through the pass," Lang said. "Close to the wall in the shadows where it will be difficult for anyone to see us."

Rosa spoke to Joaquin in Apache and the boy nodded.

"We'll ride about a mile and then walk the rest of the way," Lang said.

Rosa nodded.

"Let's get moving then," Lang said.

Johnson was bored to death on night watch. Twice he almost fell asleep. Even the several cups of coffee he drank couldn't keep him awake. Not that he actually thought anyone would be traveling through the pass at this hour, but if George knew he was sleeping on lookout, he would kill him for sure, and he'd never get to spend his share of the money.

To ease the boredom and keep himself awake, Johnson

decided to take a short ride along the ridge. For once the night air was warmer and the sky was bright and clear. The three-quarter full moon provided enough light to navigate the road along the cliffs without worry.

He rode about a mile and then dismounted.

The pass below was winding and narrow.

And then the unbelievable happened.

When Johnson looked ninety feet below the cliffs, he saw Emmet Lang riding a horse.

Chapter Fifty-Three

Another hundred yards or so, the pass took a winding route and narrowed considerably. That's where they would dismount and walk close to the canyon wall in the shadows.

He didn't really expect to see a lookout, but . . .

Lang's right rib was suddenly on fire. A fraction of a second later, the loud crack of a rifle shot resounded throughout the canyon walls.

The horse bucked in panic. Lang was thrown out of the saddle and fell against the canyon wall.

Behind his horse, Lang saw Rosa's horse buck and snort and he shouted, "Get down and hug the wall."

Rosa threw Joaquin to the ground, jumped off the horse, and shoved Joaquin against the canyon wall.

"Stay there and don't move," Lang said.

He looked up and didn't see anybody, but a moment later he heard the faint noise of a horse riding away.

Lang stood up, ignored the pain and blood streaming down from his ribs, and mounted his horse.

"Don't move," he told Rosa.

"Wait," Rosa shouted as Lang raced away.

In a panic, Johnson rode as fast as his horse could run back to the cabins. He knew his shot did no real damage as he heard Lang call out to the woman, and he wasn't sticking around to take on Emmet by his lonesome.

He raced to the point where the secret path from the canyon below led up to the flat ground, then turned left and rode the two miles to the hideaway cabins.

Lang raced along the canyon floor for about two miles. The horse was up to the mark. Mr. Daves knew how to raise a horse. Some day he would return and thank the man properly.

He slowed the horse to a stop a few feet from the dirt incline that led to the top of the cliff and to flat ground.

Lang rubbed the horse's neck and said, "See that path? We have to go up there."

The horse responded to Lang's touch by whinnying softly.

"I know," Lang said. "I don't fancy it myself, but we got no choice in the matter."

He yanked the reins and the horse started a slow ascent up the path. Midway up the path, it steepened, and the horse nearly lost his footing. Lang had to pull hard on the reins to keep the horse steady.

"The worst is over. Let's go," Lang said.

The horse took the last forty-five feet without incident and rose over the top with flared nostrils.

Lang held the horse steady for a moment while he got his bearings.

Directly west were the cabins. He could see the red dots of lanterns.

He rubbed the horse's neck.

"Got your wind?" Lang said.

The horse snorted.

"Me, too," Lang said.

He yanked the reins, and the horse responded by breaking into a flat-out run.

It was two miles to the cabins. The horse kept his pace the entire time until Lang brought him to a stop a hundred feet from the cabin where a horse was tied to a post and a lantern on the porch was lit.

A window broke. The barrel of a rifle poked out through the broken glass.

Lang pulled his Colt revolver and cocked the hammer.

"How are you at stairs?" Lang said to his horse.

The horse flared his nostrils.

"Show me," Lang said.

With the reins in his left hand, Lang brought the horse to a full run right to the stairs of the porch, where he took the four steps in one bound. Without breaking stride, the horse simply flattened the door and roared into the cabin.

Curly Johnson was at the window with a look of shock and disbelief on his face.

Smiley Hatfield was at the other window. He turned and ran to the back door of the cabin.

"Emmet?" Johnson said in disbelief at seeing Lang mounted on a horse inside the cabin.

Lang aimed the Colt and shot Johnson in the chest. The rifle slipped from Johnson's grasp as he fell to his knees.

"It weren't my doing," Johnson gasped.

"Maybe not, but you would have killed me anyway," Lang said.

Lang cocked the Colt and shot Johnson a second time in the chest and he fell over dead to the floor.

He turned the horse and road through the cabin to the open back door. There were four wood steps and the horse jumped over them to the ground.

The ground was illuminated enough by the moon for Lang to see Hatfield running from the cabin. He was about two hundred feet away and Lang yanked on the reins and the horse gave chase.

Within seconds, Lang was directly behind Smiley Hatfield.

Realizing he was beaten, Hatfield slowed to a stop. He tossed his rifle away and slowly lowered himself to his knees.

Lang rode the horse in a circle around Hatfield a few times and then stopped, facing him.

"It was all George's doing," Hatfield said.

"I know that," Lang said. "Where is he?"

"I don't know," Hatfield said. "He ran out the back door as soon as Curly rode in from his lookout. Are you going to kill me now?"

Lang sighed, then cocked the hammer of his Colt revolver and shot Hatfield in the chest just above the heart.

"Yes," Lang said. "I am."

Hatfield looked at Lang.

"No hard feelings," Hatfield said.

Lang cocked the hammer and shot Hatfield a second time, and he fell over dead.

"None," Lang said.

He opened the gate on the Colt, removed the four spent cartridges, and reloaded.

He looked back at the cabins. Just the one had light in the windows. He rode back to the dozen cabins and slowly passed each one without seeing any sign of George.

At the last cabin, Lang turned the horse around and stopped.

"George," Lang said loudly. "Let's settle this like men. Just you and me."

Lang dismounted and walked the horse to the post at the rear of the cabin where Johnson lay dead inside.

He sat on the small porch and rolled a cigarette. He lit it with a wood match from his shirt pocket.

The night air was cooler than earlier and dew was on the grass. Dawn would break within the hour and the moon was close to the horizon.

Lang inhaled on the cigarette and scanned the area behind

the cabins. There were four outhouses placed between the cabins about thirty feet behind them.

When the cigarette was spent, Lang tossed it away and stood up. He drew the Colt, cocked the hammer, and stepped off the back porch.

He walked left to the outhouse closest to him and stood a few feet from the door. Tense seconds ticked off before Lang reached for the door with his left hand and yanked it open.

The outhouse was empty.

He walked to the last outhouse on his left and stood before the closed door.

With a quick jerk on the door, he opened it and it was also empty.

Lang turned to his right and slowly walked to the third outhouse. Just as he reached the door, George opened the door to the fourth outhouse and opened fire with a rifle.

Lang spun to face George, and the bullet struck him high on the left side of his chest and exited his upper back. The force of the bullet knocked him to the ground as George fired several more times, each bullet passing over Lang's head.

"Damn you, Emmet," George shouted. "Just damn you all to hell."

Lang aimed his Colt carefully and squeezed the trigger.

A large hole appeared in George's chest, and for a moment he was still. Then, as blood appeared on his shirt, the rifle fell from George's hands.

"Dammit, Emmet, ya kilt me," George said as he slumped to his knees.

"Not yet," Lang said as he got to his feet. "Can you stand?"

"I don't think so. That bullet tore up my insides something fierce," George said.

"I hate to shoot a man like he was a sick old dog," Lang said. "Pick up the rifle and get to your feet."

"Give me a minute to get my wind, Emmet," George said.

Lang holstered his Colt and waited.

George reached for the rifle and used it as a crutch to stand up. Blood ran from the hole in his chest.

"Are you ready then?" Lang asked.

George took a deep breath and nodded.

For a moment they looked at each other.

Then George cocked the lever of the Winchester, but before he could fire, Lang drew the Colt, cocked and fired, and blew George off his feet.

Lang gently replaced the Colt and walked to George. Surprisingly, the man was still alive.

Gasping, George looked up at Lang.

"I'm kilt for sure now, Emmet," George said.

"Don't hold it against me," Lang said.

"I won't," George said. "I guess I had it coming."

A moment later, George closed his eyes and his chest went still.

"Damn it, George," Lang said.

Chapter Fifty-Four

Following Lang's tracks, Rosa and Joaquin rode their horse along the canyon floor.

After about two miles, the tracks ended abruptly.

Rosa dismounted to look around.

"Maybe the horse grew wings like Pegasus?" Rosa said aloud in English.

Joaquin dismounted and looked up at the path to the top of the canyon.

"He went here," Joaquin said in Apache.

Rosa stood beside the boy and eyed the tracks he'd pointed out.

"Yes, he did," she said.

"We should follow," Joaquin said.

Rosa nodded.

"Go," she said. "I'll follow you with the horse."

Joaquin turned and started up the path.

Rosa took the reins, led the horse to the incline, and slowly they followed the boy. "This is a secret pass?" Rosa said aloud in English. "No wonder it's a secret. You can't get to it."

Halfway up the path, the incline steepened and the horse froze in place.

Rosa turned and faced the horse. "I don't want to go either," she said. "But if you don't, I will make steaks out of you."

She tugged hard on the reins, and the horse mustered its courage and moved forward. Once over the hump of the steep incline, the path was easier to travel. They reached the top where Joaquin was waiting for them.

The boy pointed. "Lights," he said in Apache.

Rosa nodded. "Lanterns," she said. "I don't hear gunshots. Get on the horse, but when I say to get off, you get off."

They mounted the horse and rode at a trot toward the lights. The moon was gone, the dawn had begun, and soon the lanterns weren't visible.

But the cabins were.

They kept riding and after three hundred yards, Rosa stopped the horse. They faced a corral, a dozen cabins, and several sheds.

A man was seated on the porch of one of the cabins. A horse was tethered to a hitching post.

"Joaquin, get off now," Rosa said. "Find a place to hide behind and don't come out until I call."

Joaquin hopped down and Rosa slowly rode forward. When she was about fifty feet away, she could see the man on the porch was Lang.

She broke the horse into a run and jumped down at the steps of the porch.

Lang was drinking coffee. Bloodstains covered his left shoulder.

"What . . . what are you doing?" Rosa asked.

"Drinking coffee and bleeding," Lang said.

"The man who shot at you?"

"Dead. So are Hatfield and George."

"The men who . . . ?"

Lang nodded.

Rosa came up to the porch and looked at Lang's shoulder.

"What was your plan, to sit here and bleed to death?" she asked.

"My plan was to wait for you to come along and stop it," Lang said.

"Look at you, you're a mess," Rosa said. "Can you stand?"

"I think so," Lang said.

He set the cup on the porch railing and slowly stood up. "Quit moving around," he said.

"I'm not," Rosa said as Lang collapsed into her arms.

Chapter Fifty-Five

"There is a dead man on the floor," Joaquin said in Apache.

"I know," Rosa said. "We'll drag him outside as soon as I get this shirt off Mr. Lang."

They had carried Lang inside and laid him on the table in the kitchen area.

She removed the scissors from her satchel and cut off his shirt. There was a hole the size of a silver dollar just under the left shoulder in his chest. The bullet appeared to have gone clear through and exited the upper back. Luckily, it didn't strike the lung. She saw another hole along the rib cage on his right side. A few ribs were probably broken.

"He's a mess," Joaquin said in Apache.

"He is," Rosa agreed. "Build a fire in the fireplace and one in the woodstove. We have to stitch him up before he bleeds to death."

While Joaquin built the fires, Rosa pumped water from the indoor pump and set a basin to boil on the woodstove. Then she dug out sewing needles, thread, whiskey, and thimble from her satchel.

"You'll have to help me," Rosa told Joaquin. "Wash your hands with soap."

"Why?" Joaquin said.

"For the same reason I make you wash your hands before you eat when you can," Rosa said.

"But I'm not going to eat Mr. Lang," Joaquin said.

Rosa pointed to the pump. "Wash," she said.

Rosa sat in the rocking chair beside a cot and kept watch over Lang. The stitching required several hours to close the wounds. Lang didn't wake up once during the procedure, although he moaned a few times. While Rosa stitched, Joaquin did his best to hold Lang steady.

Afterward, she made coffee and took a cup with her to the rocking chair.

Joaquin was outside digging graves for the dead men. She should be helping him, but shortly after putting Lang to bed, he developed a fever.

She filled a basin with cold water and used a towel to wipe his face and chest with the water to try to break the fever.

After several hours, Joaquin came in through the back door.

"The holes are dug," he said in Apache.

"I'll help you carry the bodies," Rosa said.

"How long will he sleep?" Joaquin asked in Apache.

"Until the fever breaks," Rosa said.

They were eating dinner at the table. There were enough supplies to last the entire winter in the cabin, but little fresh meat. Joaquin hunted a pair of rabbits and Rosa made stew.

"Will he die?" Joaquin asked.

"No. He is a strong man. He won't die," Rosa said.

"But he can't ride?"

"After he wakes up, he will be weak for a few days," Rosa said. "He's lost a lot of blood. He'll need rest and food."

"I'll sit with him so you can sleep," Joaquin said.

There was a pocket watch on the fireplace mantel that probably belonged to one of the three men.

She showed the watch to Joaquin and explained to him that

when both arrows pointed north to the number twelve, he was to wake her.

Rosa sat on the chair on the porch and drank coffee. She had the coffee pot beside her feet and the pocket watch on the railing.

Lang's Colt revolver rested on her lap. His Winchester rifle leaned against the porch railing.

She sipped coffee and watched the moonlit area in front of the cabin. Soft mist rose off the grass as dew settled on the ground and created fog.

She reached for the pocket watch to check the time. It was just a few minutes before three in the morning.

She looked at the moon. In two nights it would be full. If Grey Wolf was still tracking them as she feared, he would strike during the silver moon phase if he had his way.

About a year ago, when he moved his men south to Arizona for the winter, they encountered several sodbusters that were just starting a farm. They were a threat to no one, yet Grey Wolf saw them as an enemy that needed to be wiped out of existence.

It was one week before the full moon cycle. Grey Wolf sent thirty men ahead and kept ten with him as he waited for the silver moon before attacking.

The farmers consisted of three men, their wives and children. They lived in tents while they broke ground with their plows.

Grey Wolf waited for the night of the full moon to attack the farmers and their families and murdered them in their sleep.

Grey Wolf scalped them all as a warning for any passing white man to heed.

Rosa sipped coffee.

If Grey Wolf was close enough, he would wait again for the silver moon to attack the cabin. It was almost a religious or spiritual ritual with him that even his men probably didn't understand.

Even so, Rosa did not waver as she kept a vigilant watch until the moon set and the sun appeared on the horizon.

Only when the sun was warming the ground and evaporating the dew and fog did she feel safe enough to go inside the cabin and sleep.

Joaquin sat in the rocking chair beside Lang's bed.

"He spoke a few times in his sleep," he said in Apache. "I don't know what he said."

"It doesn't matter," Rosa said as she felt Lang's face. "His fever has broken."

"Go sleep," Joaquin said. "I'll watch him."

"If he wakes up, you get me," Rosa said.

Joaquin nodded.

Rosa kissed Joaquin on his forehead, then took the cot near the fireplace and was asleep in a matter of seconds.

Chapter Fifty-Six

"What are you doing?" Rosa asked when she awoke and saw Lang seated in the rocking chair beside her bed.

Lang held up his coffee cup, and then removed the cigarette between his lips. "Drinking coffee, smoking a cigarette, and watching you sleep," he said. "Which is a hell of a lot more fun than bleeding to death."

Rosa sat up on the bed.

"Joaquin was supposed to wake me if you got up."

"My Spanish isn't so good anymore, but I told him not to."

"You shouldn't be up," she said. "You'll open your wounds."

"They won't open from just sitting in a chair," Lang said. "The coffee is fresh."

"Where is Joaquin?"

"Out back skinning a hare," Lang said. "I planned to make stew."

"You planned?" Rosa said as she stood up.

She went to the kitchen area, cranked the water pump several times, and stuck her face under the cold water. She grabbed a towel beside the pump, wiped her face dry, and then filled a cup with coffee.

Lang stood up from the rocking chair.

"It's a beautiful afternoon," he said. "Let's sit outside."

They went outside to the porch and took chairs facing the afternoon sun.

Lang pulled out his tobacco pouch and rolled a cigarette.

"I can ride tomorrow," he said.

"You still look pale," Rosa said.

"No choice," Lang said. "We can't go back and we can't stay here. Our only option is to ride to Cody as planned."

"How many days' ride?"

"Two and a bit."

"If your wounds open up on the trail, it will be difficult to stop them from bleeding."

"Like I said, no choice," Lang said. "Unless you'd like to stick around and wait for Grey Wolf to join us on the porch for tea and cake?"

Rosa grinned at Lang's remark. "No, I would not."

"Me neither."

She stood up. "I'm going to check on Joaquin," she said.

After waking up and discovering that Lang's horse had been stolen during the night, Cox took no chances. He packed whatever supplies he could carry and Lang's saddlebags onto his horse and cut the mule loose.

He rode hard, free from the bonds of two animals in tow. By midday, the day before, he'd come across Grey Wolf's dead horse. The son of a bitch had put it down with the knife and then carved steaks out of him. Cox rode until dark and then for an hour afterward before making camp.

In the morning, he picked up Grey Wolf's trail. He was less than twelve hours behind the Apache.

He needed to stay close. Lang's horse was powerful, and Cox could easily be outdistanced if he slacked off. When he made camp, Cox built a fire for coffee and to cook, as he knew Grey Wolf was through playing games now and had no desire to kill him, at least not yet.

Lang was Grey Wolf's priority, to kill the outlaw and probably his wife as well, but not the boy. Once Grey Wolf had his son, he would return for Cox.

That gave Cox a temporary advantage.

He needed to make up as much ground on Grey Wolf as he could to capitalize on that advantage.

Grey Wolf stopped to make camp at the mouth of the pass in the Big Horn Mountains. Lang's tracks were no more than two days' ride ahead of him. Earlier, he'd caught a prairie chicken. As it cooked in the fire, he wondered what destination the outlaw had in mind.

Several summers ago, he and his men rode through the Big Horn Mountains to hunt bison that roamed the valley between the ranges. There was nothing else in those mountains. Not even the railroad wanted to build a route through them, they were so desolate.

Once the outlaw discovered he and his wife couldn't escape by railroad, they'd taken to the mountains.

It wouldn't do them a bit of good.

By the silver moon, he would be upon them, have his son by his side once again, and his honor and heart would be full.

Then he and his son would hunt down the lawman dogging him, and his son would have the honor of taking his scalp as a prize.

Lang had them move to the next cabin on the left so they could lock the doors. They took most of the supplies with them. The kitchen had a root cellar where they found a fresh sack of potatoes and carrots. Rosa used the potatoes and carrots to make a rabbit stew.

After dinner, Rosa and Lang sat on the porch where the night air was cooler.

"I am tired," Rosa said.

"Get some sleep," Lang said. "I'll keep watch for a while."

"You can't . . ."

"I'm fine," Lang said. "I'll sleep in the morning."

"I won't sleep long," Rosa said.

She kissed him lightly on the lips.

"I will make you a pot of coffee before I go to bed," she said.

Lang nodded. "We'll leave tomorrow night," he said. "For Cody."

Rosa stood up and reached for the door, then paused and looked at Lang.

"I don't want to lose you," she said. Then she grinned and said, "Even if you are a lazy man."

Chapter Fifty-Seven

Lang sipped hot coffee and watched the well-lit grounds around the cabin.

The moon was close to full. Tomorrow night, it would reach its zenith and stay that way for several nights following.

In his gut, he knew Grey Wolf was on their trail.

He'd learned to trust his gut during the war. Even if you couldn't see, hear, or smell the Johnny Rebs, you somehow knew they were there in the trees or over the next hill, waiting to attack.

The hairs on the back of your neck tingled. Your hearing and eyesight became more acute. Every fiber in your body went on high alert. Then your senses proved correct when the attack came.

That's how he felt now as he sat on the porch.

He rolled a cigarette and drank another cup of coffee.

The night air was hot, dense with moisture. Fog started to form in the grass. Dew glistened in the moonlight.

He began to sweat.

Salt got into his eyes and stung.

The fog grew denser and obstructed his view of the land.

Sweat rolled down his face, and he wiped it away with the sleeve of his shirt.

Silence enveloped him. Even the peepers and frogs went still and quiet.

Lang watched the fog swirl around the land. The hairs on the back of his neck tingled. He stood up from the chair and placed his hands on the railing.

He couldn't hear a sound.

He watched the fog.

It hovered several feet above the ground and then slowly parted.

The soft noise of horses riding in the distance sounded. It grew louder. Lang squinted at the part in the fog. A squadron of Confederate soldiers riding in a V formation charged out of the fog directly at him.

The rider leading the charge wore the uniform of a Confederate captain and he held his sword pointed at Lang.

The squadron rode closer. The noise of the horses was like booming thunder.

Lang picked up the Winchester rifle and cocked the lever. He ignored the pain in his left shoulder and took careful aim at the Confederate captain. Just before he squeezed the trigger, the face of the Confederate captain became the face of Grey Wolf, the sword a tomahawk.

Grey Wolf snarled fiercely as he threw the tomahawk at Lang.

Lang flinched, and the vision vanished in a blink. He lowered the rifle, took his chair, and sighed openly with relief.

His fever had returned, and he felt as if he was standing naked in the hot sun.

Lang checked the pocket watch. Two hours to daybreak. He filled the cup with lukewarm coffee and then rolled a cigarette.

"Let him come," he said softly.

Chapter Fifty-Eight

Grey Wolf entered the box canyon just after dawn and followed the outlaw's tracks. He was not far ahead anymore, no more than a day and a half, if that.

As he rode, the canyon appeared to narrow.

Perhaps the outlaw knew a way through the mountains, or possibly he'd established a secret hideout for himself.

It didn't matter to Grey Wolf what the outlaw's plan was. It wouldn't be long before he overtook him and his deceiving wife.

All that mattered to him at this point was the return of his son.

How that happened at this point, he didn't really care.

Cox followed the tracks into the Big Horn Mountains.

After entering a canyon, he dismounted for a closer look.

The tracks left by Lang and the woman were three or four days old.

Grey Wolf was riding Lang's horse, of that Cox had no doubt, and the tracks weren't more than twelve hours old.

Cox mounted his horse and continued riding along the winding path through the canyons.

Why here? Why this long trek into the Big Horn Mountains?

Lang didn't ride all this way by accident. He had some plan or goal in mind.

He had to be protecting the woman and boy from Grey Wolf.

Why else would he stick with them for weeks and ride hundreds of miles into the mountains of Wyoming?

Cox paused briefly around noon to rest his horse and eat a cold lunch of jerky and water. It occurred to him that he had never been in the Big Horn Mountains before. He had no idea where this canyon led, if, in fact, it led anywhere.

Cox mounted his horse and rubbed his neck.

"Let's go find out," he said aloud.

"You have a fever," Rosa said when she came out to the porch shortly after dawn.

"I'm all right," Lang said. "It broke during the night."

"Are you hungry?"

"Yes."

"I'll fix breakfast and then I want to check your wounds."

"Where is the boy?"

"He went to find eggs."

"Something I need to tell you," Lang said. "I found the money we stole from Alfred Wallace in a metal box under one of the beds in the other cabin. There's thirty-eight-thousand dollars in it. I want you to take it and use it to give the boy a good life in California."

"That money doesn't belong to us," Rosa said.

"It belongs to nobody," Lang said. "Wallace stole it in the first place. There is no one to return it to. Do something good with it, for you and the boy."

"We'll talk about it later, after we eat and I check your wounds," Rosa said.

Shirtless, Lang sat in the chair on the porch. Rosa removed the wrapping from his ribs she'd made by tearing a bed sheet into strips. Lang winced as she gently touched the bruised, purple area of his top three ribs.

"You were lucky the bullet didn't enter the rib cage," Rosa said.

Joaquin came onto the porch with a basin of hot water and set it on the deck.

"Get the whiskey and a clean rag," Rosa told Joaquin in Apache.

The boy nodded and returned to the cabin.

Rosa inspected the stitches in Lang's chest and back.

"Not much leakage," she said.

Joaquin returned with the whiskey bottle and several strips of the torn sheet.

Rosa poured some whiskey on a strip of the cloth and then dabbed Lang's wounds to wipe away the dried blood. "At least it hasn't opened up," she said. "Let that dry and I'll wash it with hot water."

Lang picked up his shirt from where he'd set it on the railing and removed his tobacco pouch and papers from a pocket.

Joaquin spoke to Rosa in Apache. She replied, and he walked off the porch and around the side of the cabin.

"He wants to hunt something for tonight," Rosa said.

Lang rolled a cigarette and lit it with a wood match. "Let's talk about the money," he said.

"I told you it doesn't belong to us," Rosa said.

"That's true at this point, but it makes no sense after all we've been through not to do something good with it," Lang said. "If we return it to the government, it will just get lumped in with the pot and get wasted on something stupid. Take the boy to San Diego, buy a little place, and see he gets a good education."

"And us?"

"If you're willing to wait three years for a good for nothing, lazy man, I'm willing to join you when I get out," Lang said.

"I'm willing," Rosa said. "I'll wash the wounds, bandage your ribs, and you can get some sleep."

"Since the boy is out hunting, maybe we could sneak off to the barn for a bit?" Lang said.

"That, my lazy man, would only start your wounds bleeding again," Rosa said. "If we're to leave in the morning, I need you in one piece."

"Wake me for dinner then," Lang said.

"Don't pout," Rosa said. "You've had plenty of me on this trip."

"Three years is a long time," Lang said.

Rosa had to grin. "Let me wrap your ribs first."

Lang stood up. "Yes, ma'am," he said.

Chapter Fifty-Nine

Grey Wolf dismounted where the outlaw's tracks ended and walked a hundred yards through the narrow canyon searching for signs.

There were none.

They couldn't have backtracked. The canyon walls were too narrow for him to have missed the tracks.

He returned to his horse, carefully looked around, and noticed the disturbed rocks and pebbles on his right. They went up the hillside of the canyon, the outlaw first, followed by his wife and son.

Grey Wolf mounted Lang's horse and guided it up the canyon wall. The powerful horse had little trouble making the ascent and within minutes was on the flat plateau above the canyon floor.

Grey Wolf dismounted and inspected the tracks.

A third horse, running fast, had come from the south and it appeared that the outlaw was in pursuit.

He inspected the tracks made by his wife and son. They came hours later.

Something happened up here.

He mounted Lang's horse and followed the tracks.

After about a mile, Grey Wolf spotted something in the distance. He dismounted again and removed the binoculars he'd taken from a soldier he'd killed when he was freed from the prison wagon.

Through the binoculars, Grey Wolf saw a string of cabins, a corral with five horses, and smoke rising from one chimney.

He packed the binoculars away in the saddlebags, rode another three quarters of a mile, and found shelter behind a large tree.

Using the binoculars again, he watched the cabins for quite a while. His patience was rewarded when he saw the outlaw and Rosa come out to the porch of a cabin. They were drinking from cups and talking.

It was as he'd believed. Rosa was with the outlaw willingly.

They talked for a while, and then the outlaw stood and removed his shirt. Joaquin came out with a basin of water and Rosa tended to what looked like several recent wounds.

Something did happen here, Grey Wolf reasoned. That's why an extra three horses resided in the corral. Lang fought with three other men and emerged the victor, if wounded.

Grey Wolf lowered the binoculars and settled against the tree to take a nap.

Night was just a few hours away, and then his spirit would be whole again.

Around sunset, Cox lost the tracks in the narrow canyon floor. Lang's, along with Grey Wolf's tracks, simply stopped.

But that wasn't possible.

Yet the tracks ended without a trace.

Once the sun had set and before the moon rose, the floor of the canyon was too dark to see anything.

Cox built a fire and put on a pot of coffee.

When it boiled, he filled his cup, sat before the fire, and lit his pipe.

Something happened here.

An attack or ambush possibly.

But that didn't explain how the tracks of the horses came to a sudden stop.

They couldn't have backtracked without his noticing it inside the narrow canyon.

Come morning, he would have to backtrack just in case, and if he found nothing, proceed forward and hope for the best.

He wasn't really hungry, but he ate a few stale biscuits and some jerky, then bedded down for the night beside the fire.

Chapter Sixty

"Whichever outlaws built this place knew what they were doing," Lang told Rosa after dinner. "The root cellar locks from the inside with two planks of wood. I want you to take the boy and some candles and spend the night there. I did some poking around, and on the back side of the cellar, there are two boards that come loose and lead to a tunnel that comes up behind the fourth outhouse. If you hear gunshots, you escape with the boy."

"But I won't—" Rosa said.

"Pack food and water for several days and bring it down with you," Lang said. "No arguments."

He went to the pantry, returned with George's Colt revolver and holster, and gave it to Rosa.

"And take this with you," he said.

Rosa stared at Lang. Her lips quivered.

"No words," Lang said. "Just do as I ask. Please."

Rosa nodded. "All right," she said softly.

"I'll be out on the porch," Lang said.

Rosa watched him strap on his gun belt, pick up the Winchester rifle, and walk to the door.

"Emmet?" Rosa said.

"It will be all right," he said and went out to the porch.

Lang rolled a cigarette and watched the moon slowly ascend in the sky. Almost a dark red when it showed itself, it slowly turned white as it rose higher in an arc and then appeared almost silver.

He pulled out the pocket watch, opened the face, and set it on the railing so he could read the time.

Beside the chair was a fresh pot of coffee and a cup.

The Winchester rifle leaned against the porch railing within arm's reach.

He smoked the cigarette with a cup of coffee.

Behind him, the lanterns inside the cabin went out.

Lang concentrated on adjusting his night vision the way he was taught in officers' training school.

He focused on the ground and avoided looking at the bright full moon.

As his eyes grew accustomed to the dark, he could almost read a newspaper by the pale moonlight.

Dew settled on the grass and glistened.

His skin felt hot and clammy.

Fog slowly formed. Thin at first, it thickened like pea soup, and visibility grew limited after a few hundred feet.

His hearing sharpened.

The fog directly ahead of him began to gently swirl.

Lang sat up in the chair and watched the fog. Illuminated by the moon, it was almost mystical in its beauty.

The fog began to slowly part about a hundred feet in front of the cabin.

Lang set the coffee cup on the porch railing and stood up.

He watched the opening.

A figure emerged, shrouded in the swirling fog.

The figure moved forward a bit and stood in the moonlight.

It was Grey Wolf. Shirtless, a tomahawk in his right hand, a long knife in the left, his face was streaked with black and white war paint. He was as fearsome a figure of a warrior as Lang had ever seen.

Lang picked up the rifle, cocked the lever, pressed the butt against his right shoulder, and took careful aim.

Grey Wolf didn't move, not even a flinch.

Lang placed his finger on the trigger, took a shallow breath, and stared at the face of Grey Wolf.

The Apache held his ground.

Lang lowered the Winchester, de-cocked it, and set it against the chair.

"Invitation accepted," he said.

He removed his shirt, placed it over the railing, and then stepped down off the porch and looked at Grey Wolf.

Grey Wolf appeared to give him a tiny head nod.

Lang removed his knife and held it in his left hand. Then he pulled his Colt revolver and held it by the barrel like a club in his right hand.

Lang and Grey Wolf eyed each other through the swirling fog.

For several moments, neither man moved.

Lang took a shallow breath and said softly, "Your party, your move."

Grey Wolf broke into a sudden run with the tomahawk held high above his head.

"She isn't yours," Lang said and charged Grey Wolf.

It only took seconds to cover the hundred feet. At the last moment, both Grey Wolf and Lang sprang up and came together.

Grey Wolf swung his tomahawk.

Lang blocked it with the butt of his Colt.

On contact, both men felt a jolt and they came apart.

They made eye contact. Their eyes showed mutual respect.

"She isn't yours," Lang said.

Grey Wolf swung the tomahawk. Lang blocked it with the butt of his Colt.

Lang slashed out with his knife several times and backed

Grey Wolf up a few feet and Grey Wolf countered by swinging the tomahawk and missing Lang's face by inches.

The see-saw battle raged on for many long minutes with neither of them gaining or giving an inch.

They came apart and stepped back.

Grey Wolf looked at the blood oozing from the stitches in Lang's left side.

"She isn't yours," Lang said.

Grey Wolf struck out with his knife. Lang blocked it with the butt of his Colt, and then Grey Wolf slashed the tomahawk directly into Lang's stitches.

Lang cried out as blood gushed, but he didn't lose focus. He swung the Colt and slapped the tomahawk from Grey Wolf's grasp.

Grey Wolf slashed Lang's right wrist with his knife and the Colt fell to the ground.

They stepped back, breathing hard, and looked at each other. They lowered their knives to their sides and for a moment they didn't move. An odd feeling of mutual respect passed between the two combatants.

Grey Wolf suddenly lurched forward and tackled Lang around the legs. Both men spilled to the ground, and Lang's knife broke loose.

They rolled and Grey Wolf jumped to his feet first. As Lang stood up, Grey Wolf moved in with his knife. He thrust it at Lang's chest. Lang caught Grey Wolf's wrists and held fast.

Grey Wolf dug in and pushed forward.

Lang dug in and held his ground.

Slowly the knife moved closer to Lang's chest.

Lang looked into Grey Wolf's eyes. "She isn't yours," he said.

Grey Wolf grunted as he pushed the knife closer to Lang's chest.

Lang looked to the ground and saw his knife just a few feet

away. He eased up a bit and allowed the knife to move closer to his chest, drawing Grey Wolf in, and then pulled forward and tossed Grey Wolf across his body to the ground.

Lang rolled to the ground, grabbed his knife, and slammed it into Grey Wolf's left hamstring muscle. "She isn't yours!" he screamed.

Lang pulled the knife out of Grey Wolf's flesh and jumped to his feet.

With blood running down the left hamstring, Grey Wolf slowly made it to his feet. He stared at Lang.

Lang received the shock of his life when Grey Wolf turned suddenly and hobbled back into the fog and disappeared.

For a moment, Lang was still. Then he replaced the knife in its sheath. He located his Colt revolver and holstered it.

Then he turned and walked to the cabin, feeling light-headed.

Just as he reached the steps, dizziness engulfed him, his head spun as if he were drunk, and he passed out cold on the porch.

Inside the root cellar, Rosa heard Lang's voice cry out in the night. She couldn't understand the words, but she knew it was him.

"I'm going to see," she told Joaquin in Apache. "You wait for me here."

She removed the two wood planks and pushed the false floorboards up and away from the opening. She took one of the two lit candles, climbed out, and stood motionless in the kitchen.

She heard nothing and pulled George's Colt from her belt and cocked the hammer.

Then she walked to the door, opened it, and found Lang passed out on the porch.

Chapter Sixty-One

"He's a mess again," Joaquin said in Apache.

"Never mind he's a mess again and fetch the hot water," Rosa said.

By lantern and candlelight, Rosa cleaned Lang's wounds with hot water and whiskey and then tightened the stitches.

"Help me get him on the bed," Rosa told Joaquin when she was satisfied the stitches would hold.

Rosa and Joaquin lifted Lang from the table and slowly carried him to the bed and gently set him down.

"Sit with him. If his fever returns, come and get me," she told Joaquin.

She went out to the porch where the Winchester rifle leaned against the chair. She picked up Lang's shirt, placed it around her shoulders, and sat in the chair. She picked up the Winchester and set it on her lap.

The wound to his leg was serious enough that had he continued the fight, it would have ended in his death.

He underestimated the outlaw, a mistake he wouldn't make a second time.

Grey Wolf returned to the horse, rode several miles to the west, and made a fire. He carried several knives and tomahawks in his saddlebags and put one of the knives into the fire to heat.

He dug out the whiskey bottle and took several gulps, then poured some over the wound. It stung, but that was nothing compared to what was to come.

He watched the fire. When the knife was hot enough, he pulled it from the fire, turned and pressed the hot steel against the wound on his left hamstring.

The flesh sizzled like beef on a fire. Grey Wolf smelled his own flesh cook as he held the knife to the wound for five seconds.

The knife fell from his grasp and, slowly, Grey Wolf lowered himself to the ground next to the fire.

A moment later, he passed out.

Rosa fell asleep with the sun on her face.

She wasn't asleep long when Joaquin came out, shook her, and told her that Lang was awake.

She went inside. Lang was more than awake. He was at the table, drinking coffee from a fresh pot.

"What are you doing?" Rosa asked, angrily.

"Having some coffee," Lang said. "Want some?"

"I don't want . . . how could you . . . what happened last night?" Rosa asked as she took a chair at the table.

"Grey Wolf," Lang said.

"I realize Grey Wolf," Rosa said. "What happened?"

"He showed up."

"No kidding. Why didn't you shoot him?"

"He didn't have a rifle," Lang said.

"So what did you do, challenge him to a fight like a couple of idiot boys in the schoolyard?"

"Something like that, only he issued the challenge," Lang said. "Have some coffee. It's fresh."

"I don't want . . . what happened to him?"

"We sort of got into it for a while. It was touch and go until I got him in the leg with my knife," Lang said.

"Then what happened?"

"He ran away."

Rosa was startled and stared at Lang.

"He ran away? Grey Wolf?" she said.

"A deep knife wound to the hamstring cripples a man," Lang said. "I guess he figured it was better to live and fight another day."

"Are you fit to ride?" Rosa asked.

Lang nodded. "I will be in a bit."

"I'll fix some breakfast and then I suggest we be on our way," Rosa said.

"Good idea," Lang said.

Grey Wolf rolled over into the cold campfire and opened his eyes. The smell of ashes stung his nose.

It took a few seconds for the pain in his leg to kick in, and then he sat up and moaned.

He waited a few minutes to allow the fire in his leg to lesson, and then he slowly stood up.

He took a few, stiff-legged steps and then checked the wound. There was no blood.

The leg would be a painful hindrance for a while, but it could have been far worse.

He rebuilt the fire and smoked his pipe before the warming flames and thought about what had happened.

The outlaw had proven to be his equal, something Grey Wolf would never have believed. But there was more to the matter than he originally believed. The outlaw had feelings for Rosa, made perfectly clear not in just the way he fought, but in his words.

"She isn't yours," the outlaw said many times.

Grey Wolf's victory in their death would be just that much sweeter.

★ ★ ★ ★ ★

Up at dawn, Cox gathered enough wood to build a fire and have some breakfast. There was some bacon left, and he cooked it with beans and a small pot of coffee. He ate a few stale biscuits softened by dunking them in coffee.

Then he walked the canyon floor and checked for tracks and signs he might have missed last night.

He returned to his campsite perplexed.

There was one cup of coffee left in the pot. He filled his cup, then stuffed his pipe and sat before the dwindling fire.

The tracks ended at his campsite. They didn't backtrack.

The only place left they could have gone was . . .

Cox stood and looked at the canyon walls.

. . . Up.

Chapter Sixty-Two

"If we travel north along the ridge, it leads to a back road out of the mountains," Lang said. "It's well hidden and only a few people know it's there."

"You said that about the pass," Rosa said. "And we had a crowd like a line for the circus."

"Under the circumstances, we have little choice," Lang said. "We'll leave at dark and travel all night. I don't think Grey Wolf is in any condition to track us."

"Don't underestimate that one," Rosa said.

They were at the table. Rosa had two loaves of bread in the oven. She stood up to check them, removed them from the oven, and set them on the counter to cool.

"Is two enough?" she asked.

"With all the food and canned goods around here, more than enough," Lang said.

"Then we should pack," Rosa said.

The cabin door was open. Joaquin stepped inside and spoke to Rosa in Apache.

Rosa looked at Lang. "He said a man is coming."

Lang stood on the porch with the Winchester rifle held loosely in his arms and watched the rider approach from a distance of about a half mile.

The rider was in no particular hurry and rode his horse at little more than a moderate walk.

Lang pulled out his tobacco pouch and rolled a cigarette. He lit it off a wood match and then picked up his coffee cup, which he had rested on the porch railing.

By the time the cigarette was finished, the rider was less than three hundred yards away and still in no hurry.

The sun was at the rider's back, and it was difficult to see his face until he was much closer.

Lang set the Winchester against the railing and waited for the man to arrive.

Finally he arrived at the hitching post near the porch steps.

"I'm US Marshal John Cox," the man said as he dismounted. "I recognize you as Emmet Lang."

"We've crossed paths before," Lang said. "I recognize your face."

"Any more of that coffee?" Cox asked.

"Plenty," Lang said.

At the table, Cox sipped coffee and listened as Rosa and Lang talked, although it was mostly Rosa who did the talking.

When she was through, Cox stuffed his pipe and lit it with a wood match Lang provided.

"Let me see if I understand this," Cox said. "Lang and his men robbed the stagecoach, but only wanted one man, this Alfred Wallace. He was an Indian Affairs agent who robbed the agency of forty thousand dollars. Your men got greedy, took all the money, and killed all the passengers, leaving you behind. They took the woman and her son and left them in the abandoned stage."

"After they violated me," Rosa added. "Don't forget that."

"Right," Cox said.

"Then along comes Lang and he rescues you and . . . I'm not clear after that part," Cox said.

"I told you, he saved me and my son from Grey Wolf," Rosa

said. "We went to Riverton, but Grey Wolf had his men burn the railroad tracks."

"And then you came here?" Cox said.

"Yes," Rosa said.

Cox looked at Lang. "Where your men happened to be hiding, and you killed them all after they ambushed you," he said. "Then Grey Wolf showed up and you wounded him and he escaped?"

Lang shrugged.

"It's true. Every word of it," Rosa said. "Emmet, show him your wounds."

"No need for that," Cox said. "I can see he's beat to hell. So after all this, you were going to ride to Cody and turn yourselves in to the army."

"Just me and my son," Rosa said. "Emmet was going to surrender to the sheriff."

Cox looked at Lang. "Why?"

"It's time," Lang said. "That's all."

"You could get three to five years for the robbery," Cox said.

Rosa stood up, went to her bed, and returned with the cashbox. She set it before Cox, sat, and said, "Not if he returns the money."

Cox opened the box and looked at the thick stacks of bills. "How much is in here?"

"Thirty-eight of the forty thousand," Lang said. "George and the boys must have spent some on their way here."

"Well, you can surrender to me," Cox said. "We'll ride to Cody, and she and the boy can be under the protection of the army until Grey Wolf is captured or killed."

"And Emmet?" Rosa asked.

"We'll proceed south to Cheyenne, where he'll stand before a federal district judge," Cox said.

"I will be allowed to testify on his behalf?" Rosa asked. "I wrote a statement, but I can write another one if necessary."

"Don't see why not," Cox said.

"We planned to leave at dusk and travel at night," Lang said. "It's an easy ride along the road and safer with Grey Wolf still around."

"Fair enough," Cox said. "Something I should tell you. I found your horse. A few days ago, Grey Wolf snuck into my camp and stole him."

"Grey Wolf is riding my horse?" Lang said.

"He didn't get your saddlebags, though," Cox said. "The contents are still intact. Thirty-five hundred dollars and a silver watch. More than enough to hire the best defense lawyers in Cheyenne."

"I'm grateful to you for that," Lang said.

"Something else," Cox said. "The horses you're riding, where did you get them?"

"We met a rancher named Daves," Lang said. "He helped us and gave us two horses."

"Grey Wolf caught up with him," Cox said. "Murdered the whole family."

Rosa gasped, got up from the table, and went out to the porch.

"I'm sorry about that news," Cox said.

"He was a good man," Lang said.

"Hey, where's the boy?" Cox asked.

"He went shopping," Lang said.

Rosa fried up the three prairie chickens Joaquin hunted and served an early dinner of the chickens, potatoes, carrots, and bread.

After dinner, Lang and Cox took coffee on the porch.

Lang rolled a cigarette. Cox smoked his pipe.

"Something happened out there on the trail," Cox said. "You

and the woman fell in love, didn't you? I can see it on both your faces."

"You say it like it was a disease," Lang said.

"Not at all," Cox said. "I'm a big believer in love."

Chapter Sixty-Three

They ate with the sun on their faces after an all-night ride along the plateau road.

"Another night's ride and we'll be in the pass," Lang said. "From there it's a half day's ride to Cody."

"We'll sleep in shifts until dark," Cox said.

"I'll need my Colt and Winchester when I stand watch," Lang said. "I'll return them when I'm relieved."

"Seeing as how we're easy prey out here in the open, I'll agree to that," Cox said.

By late afternoon, all four of them were wide awake and ready to go. They ate a quick supper and were in the saddle two hours before sunset.

"Around two or three this morning, we should start down to the pass through the canyon," Lang said. "We should clear it by dawn, and then it's not far to Cody."

They stopped after dark to rest the horses and eat a cold snack.

As they continued to ride, the full moon slowly rose into the sky.

Joaquin spoke in Apache.

"What did he say?" Cox asked.

"The moon," Rosa said. "He called it the silver moon rising."

Cox looked at the moon.

"Is that some Apache ritual thing?" he asked.

"Only to Grey Wolf," Rosa said. "It is the time he likes best to kill."

"No sign of him dogging us," Cox said. "And he's outnumbered and wounded."

"Another few hours and we can descend into the pass," Lang said.

"It's single file until we clear the canyon floor," Lang said when they reached the spot of the descent.

"I'll go first," Cox said. "Lang, you follow and then the woman and boy."

The descent was gentle and went on for about a mile until they reached the canyon floor.

"We'll give the horses a breather and us, too," Cox said. "Long enough to make a pot of coffee."

"Is a fire wise?" Rosa asked.

"If he's dogging us, he won't need a fire to see," Cox said. "This damn moon is so bright it casts shadows."

Rosa built a small fire and boiled a pot of coffee.

Lang rolled a cigarette and took a cup, then dug out his silver pocket watch. "If we didn't stop but one more time to rest the horses, we could be in Cody by noon," he said.

Rosa filled a cup with coffee and gave it to Cox.

"Obliged," he said. "We'll stop at daybreak for a quick bite and to rest the horses as you said."

The canyon walls narrowed. The moon lit the walls and floor so brightly, they could clearly see each other's faces.

Lang's eyes constantly scanned the canyon walls for signs of Grey Wolf, but there were none. The Apache was too experienced a fighter to expose himself to his enemy unless it was deliberate.

Several hours before daybreak, Lang stopped his horse.

Behind him, Rosa stopped hers.

In the lead, Cox stopped his horse and turned in the saddle.

"What?" Cox asked.

"Be still a moment," Lang said.

Cox looked at Lang as Lang appeared to stare straight ahead. Then Lang lifted his eyes to scan the cliffs.

Cox turned and looked up.

A soft thud sounded and a hole appeared in his chest. A fraction of a second later, the crack of a rifle shot echoed throughout the canyon as Cox fell from his horse.

Lang's horse bucked up and struck Rosa's horse behind him. Lang fell from the saddle and rolled out of the way of his frightened horse.

Against the canyon wall, Lang looked up and saw Grey Wolf, tomahawk in hand, charging down. His face was decorated in war paint, his scowl fierce. A makeshift splint was on his left leg and even though he moved with a limp, his charge was swift.

Rosa and Joaquin were frozen on their horse.

By the time Lang stood up, Grey Wolf was halfway down the ridge.

Lang looked for Cox. He was on the ground in front of his panicked horse. Lang spotted the Winchester rifle in its sleeve on Cox's horse and tried to grab it, but the horse reared up and bucked wildly.

Grey Wolf screamed as he neared the bottom of the canyon floor.

Lang grabbed the reins of Cox's horse and pulled hard to get him under control, then grabbed the Winchester from the sleeve.

Grey Wolf touched down twenty feet from Lang.

Lang turned and cocked the lever of the Winchester.

Grey Wolf roared as he charged Lang with his tomahawk.

With barely three feet between them, Lang pulled the trigger and a hole appeared in Grey Wolf's chest.

Grey Wolf stopped as if he'd hit a wall and looked at the bloody hole.

Lang cocked the lever a second time.

Grey Wolf raised the tomahawk over his head and screamed his war cry with furious anger.

Lang fired the Winchester and blew a second hole in Grey Wolf's chest just under the heart.

Grey Wolf looked at Lang. The tomahawk fell from his grasp. He looked down at the two gaping holes in his chest. He made eye contact with Lang for a few seconds, and then he slowly sank to his knees and fell to the ground.

"I told you, she isn't yours," Lang said.

A moment later, Grey Wolf's eyes closed and he went still.

Lang stepped over Grey Wolf and knelt beside Cox.

"He's still alive," Lang said to Rosa. "Take the saddle off my horse."

Rosa dismounted, looked at Grey Wolf, and then went to Lang's horse. "What are you . . ." she said, but Lang was gone.

Lang raced up the side of the canyon wall to the plateau, where he found his horse tied to a nearby tree. He untied the reins and rubbed the horse's nose.

"Remember me?" he said.

Lang mounted his horse and rode him down the side of the wall to the canyon floor and dismounted beside Rosa.

He immediately removed Grey Wolf's saddle and replaced it with the one provided by Daves.

"I need to get the marshal to Cody before he bleeds out and dies," he said. "Follow as best you can."

Lang opened the saddlebags on Cox's horse, retrieved his gun belt and strapped it on, then placed his Winchester in the saddle sleeve.

"Help me get him in the saddle," Lang said.

Lang and Rosa lifted Cox onto the saddle of Lang's horse.

Lang found some rope in Cox's saddlebags and cut strips to tie Cox's hands to the horn.

"When you come out of the canyon, stay northwest until you reach the road to Cody," Lang said.

Rosa nodded, and then kissed Lang. "We'll be there," she said.

He mounted his tall horse, yanked the reins, and rode away hard.

Chapter Sixty-Four

When Rosa and Joaquin rode into the town of Cody in the late afternoon, it was as if every citizen of the town was on the street.

Joaquin rode Cox's horse.

Rosa didn't know where else to go, so she found the sheriff's office and dismounted in front of it.

The sheriff was out front.

"Are you Rosa Escalante, wife of Grey Wolf?" the sheriff asked.

"I am," Rosa said. "This is my son, Joaquin."

"I have orders to escort you to the army post a mile outside of town," the sheriff said.

"I'm Major Thornton, commander of this outpost."

Rosa looked at the major. "Rosa Escalante. This is Joaquin, my son."

"You're a brave woman, Rosa Escalante," Thornton said.

"Where are the marshal and Mr. . . . ?"

"Lang?" Thornton said.

Rosa looked at Thornton. "He told me his name when he surrendered his gun," Thornton said.

Rosa nodded.

"The marshal is recovering from surgery and Mr. Lang is in the brig," Thornton said.

"Brig?"

"Another name for jail."

"Can I see him?" Rosa asked.

"Yes," Thornton said. "Afterward, we have a room for you and your son where you can take a bath and then join me for dinner."

The brig consisted of a railroad-style building that held six small cells. Just one was occupied.

Rosa stood before the occupied cell and looked at Lang.

He grinned at her. "Well, we made it," he said.

"Except that I'm to have a fancy dinner with the major, and you're in a cage like a wild beast," Rosa said.

"I best get used to it," Lang said. "A cage will be my home for the next three years or so."

"I will wait for you," Rosa said.

"Are you sure?"

"I am sure."

"Where is Joaquin?"

"Taking a bath," Rosa said. "After that, he will visit the army doctor and then the army barber."

"Make sure he learns English in California and gets an education," Lang said. "You don't want him to grow up to be a lazy man."

Rosa's lips began to quiver as she nodded. "I will make sure," she said.

A soldier appeared behind her.

"Ma'am, the major requests your presence," he said.

"It isn't the envy of Paris, but it's the best selection in dresses they had in town," Thornton said.

Rosa looked at the selection of dresses and shoes on the bed of the guest room Thornton had allocated for her. There was a large wrapped box beside the bed.

"The box contains private garments," Thornton explained.

"I have money to pay for this," Rosa said.

"Not necessary," Thornton said. "Dinner is at seven at my table. Your bath is ready. I'll see you then."

Sixty soldiers stood at attention when Major Thornton escorted Rosa and Joaquin into the post mess hall.

"At ease, men," Thornton said as he walked Rosa and Joaquin to his table.

Two officers stood at their chairs.

"This is Captain McNeal and First Lieutenant Carter," Thornton said.

"How do you do," Rosa said.

Thornton held the chair for Rosa and after she sat, McNeal, Carter, and Joaquin took their places.

"I must say that with a haircut and some new clothes, your son is quite a handsome boy," Thornton said. "Does he speak English?"

"Joaquin speaks Spanish, French, and Apache, but very little English," Rosa said.

Thornton looked at Joaquin and spoke in French. "My mother was French, and she taught me the language as a boy. Never forget the languages you learn, Joaquin."

Joaquin nodded. "I won't," he said in French.

Soldiers acting as waiters served a dinner of roast beef and chicken.

"Major Thornton, while we are eating such fine food, what is Mr. Lang having for dinner?" Rosa asked.

"Good point," Thornton said. He looked at First Lieutenant Carter. "Would you find out, Lieutenant?"

"Yes, sir."

★ ★ ★ ★ ★

"You're a lucky man, Marshal," the post doctor said as he cleaned and dressed Cox's wound.

"Never mind the lucky man crap," Cox said. "I'm hungry and I want to eat, and after I eat, I want to see Major Thornton."

The doctor nodded. "All right, but don't go bouncing around," he said.

Cox was sitting up in bed, smoking his pipe after a dinner of roast beef and chicken.

There was a knock on the bedroom door. It opened and Major Thornton walked in and said, "You wanted to see me, Marshal?"

"Pull up a chair," Cox said. "We need to have us a talk."

Chapter Sixty-Five

At sunrise, Lang was served breakfast in his cell. Afterward, he was escorted to the bathhouse for a shave and a bath and was surprised to find clean clothing waiting for him when he got out of the tub.

Two soldiers stayed with him the entire time. When he was dressed, one soldier said, "We're going to see the major."

"I figured," Lang said.

The soldiers escorted Lang past the major's office to the infirmary building.

Major Thornton was waiting in the small lobby. "You men are dismissed," he said to the two escorts.

"You sent for me, Major?" Lang asked.

"Actually, Marshal Cox did," Thornton said. "He's in his room."

So were Rosa and Joaquin. She wore a stylish blue dress with new shoes. Her hair was done in a long braid. The boy wore new pants, shirt, and shoes. They stood beside the window to the left of the bed.

Cox was sitting up and smoking his pipe.

Thornton stood beside the bed.

Lang stood at the foot of the bed and looked at Cox.

"I've been a lawman my entire life," Cox said. "This was my last official act of duty. I'm going to retire and then visit my daughters and their nincompoop husbands as soon as I get out of here. Then maybe . . . I don't know. But I got a second chance, and I'm going to make the most of it. My father used to say when I was a boy that a man can't live in the present and look to have a future if he lives in the past with ghosts."

Cox paused to shake his pipe out into a large ashtray on the table beside the bed. He stuffed fresh tobacco into the pipe and lit it with a wood match.

"In the meantime, I'll be in this bed another week according to the doctor," Cox said. "I'm going to use that time to write my report. It will be extensive in detail. In that report, I'm going to write how I tracked the outlaw Emmet Lang and the Apache war chief known as Grey Wolf clear across kingdom come until I found them dead by each other's hands in the Big Horn Mountains. It's also going to say how the wife and son of Grey Wolf are in whereabouts unknown. Probably dead."

Lang looked at Rosa, but she had no expression on her face.

"The other thing my report will say is how I was ambushed and shot, and a man named Daves came to my aid and saved my life," Cox said. "Isn't that right, Major?"

Thornton looked at Lang. "That's correct, Marshal," Thornton said.

"In conclusion, my report will say I was able to return thirty of the forty thousand dollars of the money stolen from one Alfred Wallace at that stage robbery," Cox said. "The other ten thousand is still missing. Probably spent."

Lang looked at Rosa. She was grinning.

"Major Thornton, do you have anything to add to my report?" Cox asked.

Thornton looked at Rosa and then turned and looked at Lang.

"Just that Mr. Daves here and his family were given an army escort to Riverton to catch the railroad west," Thornton said.

Cox nodded to Lang. "Good day, Mr. Daves," he said.

Thornton escorted Lang, Rosa, and Joaquin to the door.

Lang paused to turn around and look at Cox.

"Like I said," Cox said. "I'm a big believer in love."

ABOUT THE AUTHOR

Ethan J. Wolfe is the author of the western novels *The Last Ride, The Regulator, The Range War of '82,* and *Murphy's Law.*